PRAISE FOR THE NEW MYSTERY SERIES
FEATURING MRS. PARGETER
FROM SIMON BRETT!

"Mrs. Pargeter is no spinster from a small English village. She is wily, earthy widow, more likely to pick a lock than knit baby clothes."
—*Washington Post Book World*

"Of the many imitations of Agatha Christie's Miss Marple, none has been quite so slippery and criminious as Melita Pargeter, a white-haired, well-heeled widow of a burglar whom Brett beguilingly introduced in 1987's *A Nice Class of Corpse.* . . . She returns in *Mrs, Presumed Dead* to expose the follies of an executive suburb."
—*Time*

"Self-contained village atmosphere, a restricted circle of suspects who slowly reveal their secrets, and breezy, witty style all contribute to a most attractive package."
—*Library Journal*

"Simon Brett's spirited new sleuth, Mrs. Melita Pargeter, remains a wily charmer, and her unorthodox methods of detection . . . are certainly entertaining."
—Marilyn Stasio, *The New York Times Book Review*

SIMON BRETT

MRS, PRESUMED DEAD

A DELL BOOK

Published by
Dell Publishing
a division of
Bantam Doubleday Dell Publishing Group, Inc.
666 Fifth Avenue
New York, New York 10103

The Trademark Dell® is registered in the U.S. Patent and Trademark Office.

ISBN: 0-440-20552-2

Reprinted by arrangement with Charles Scribner's Sons.

Printed in the United States of America

February 1990

10 9 8 7 6 5 4 3 2 1

OPM

MRS,
PRESUMED
DEAD

CHAPTER ONE

The murderer looked down at the body lying neatly in the middle of its polythene sheet, and indulged in a moment of self-congratulation. It had really been remarkably easy once the decision had been made. The polythene sheet over the thick carpet had been a bonus, no great surprise that it should have been there, considering all the packing of the last few days, but nonetheless a bonus. Not only would it minimise the likelihood of detection, it also fitted in with the murderer's instinctive fastidiousness.

In the event, there had been little mess. The woman on the polythene sheet lay in a posture that could at a cursory glance have been mistaken for sleep. Properly surprised by the suddenness of the attack, she had gone to her death

1

with the docility which, to outsiders, had characterised her life.

Only a close inspection would have revealed the thin red weal of bruising on the stark whiteness of her neck. And the curtain of reddish hair would have had to be lifted to uncover the livid face with its startled eyes and its engorged tongue parting puffy lips.

The murderer, secure in rubber gloves, dropped the stretched cricket club tie on top of its victim, then wrapped the convenient polythene around the body and sealed it with sticky tape. Like that, the corpse lost its last residual connection with humanity and became just another package ready for removal, along with the tea-chests of newspaper-wrapped china and the stout cardboard boxes full of ornaments, which waited in obedient rows along the wall of that sitting-room.

Surprised by a flicker of anxiety, the murderer's eyes darted to the large picture window, but the thick Dralon curtains were reassuringly closed. They had been expensively tailored for the space and admitted no sliver of light to the outside world. No one else on the estate could even know whether the lights were on or off.

The anxiety gave way to the return of self-congratulation. Yes, it really had been remarkably easy.

And necessary. Regrettable, but necessary. The risk of discovery had been too great, and once that risk had become known, ordinary human considerations had ceased to be relevant. A kind of mechanistic change had come over both of them. From that moment they had ceased to be people, become abstract figures, archetypes—murderer and victim.

Even now it was done, the situation remained clinical, objective. In the murderer's mind there was no guilt, only a process of logical assessment, of working out the odds against being detected as the perpetrator of the crime.

And at that moment those odds seemed comfortingly long. Yes, in with an excellent chance of getting away with it.

Bolstered by this thought, the murderer's mind now felt ready to address that problem which has always proved a much greater deterrent to homicide than any moral or religious qualm—how to dispose of the body.

CHAPTER TWO

Smithy's Loam was a development of six executive homes which had been built some five years previously in the outer commuter belt of Surrey, and whose history was interchangeable with that of many such executive estates. Its developer had bought up a dilapidated Victorian rectory, obtained planning permission with the help of a fellow member of the Rotary Club who happened to be on the local council, demolished the rectory and divided its three acres into six plots tastefully scattered around a central green. To give these outer-suburban dwellings with their pale new brick an air of rustic permanence, he had sought out an appropriate name and, prompted by someone's vague recollection that there might have been a forge on the site

4

before the rectory, had dubbed the development Smithy's Loam. Then, having made a killing on the project, he had taken early retirement to Tenerife, where he proceeded very slowly and pleasurably to drink himself to death.

In the five years of its existence Smithy's Loam had seen a good few changes of ownership. Though the houses were well up in the market, four-bedroomed dwellings whose comfortably accelerating prices excluded most first-time buyers, the sort of people who bought them, rising executives in their thirties and forties, were vulnerable to sudden moves. Keeping themselves on the upward graph of success depended on seizing their opportunities when they arose, taking on new jobs, being transferred at short notice to new areas. So the appearance of removal lorries in Smithy's Loam was not an unfamiliar sight.

What was unusual, though, thought Vivvi Sprake, as she looked out of the front window of Number Three ("Haymakers") across the immaculate central green to the lorry outside Number Six ("Acapulco"), was for the new residents not to be present when their furniture was unloaded.

For that was what appeared to be happening. Without, as she kept telling herself, being nosy, Vivvi kept a fairly close eye on what went on in the close (oh no, mustn't call it a "close"—Nigel said "close" was common). And she was sure the new resident hadn't arrived yet.

She ran through the sequence of events. Theresa Cotton, when she had come round to say goodbye on the Monday evening, had said she was just about to leave. On the Tuesday morning her removal lorry had arrived at the unoccupied house, been loaded with its contents and set off on the long journey North to the Cottons' new home. And now, on the Wednesday morning, the new resident's belongings were being unloaded into "Acapulco." But the new resident herself had not yet put in an appearance.

Somehow this upset Vivvi's sense of rightness. Removal firms were so unreliable, surely most people would want to be on the spot to see that things were put in the correct places? Anyway, being around and making endless cups of tea for the removal men seemed to Vivvi an essential rite of passage, a necessary part of the process of moving into a new home. The new resident's absence disturbed her. It opened up the possibility that there might be other ways in which the newcomer would not conform to the usages of Smithy's Loam. And to Vivvi, herself always working so hard, at her husband Nigel's insistence—so many things are so difficult when you marry an older husband—to do the right thing, this prospect was doubly irritating.

By half-past twelve the new owner of "Acapulco" still hadn't turned up, though the removers seemed to be down to the smallest items and had the air of men about to fold up their final blankets before going off to the pub. Vivvi sighed with annoyance and went into the kitchen to make herself a cottage cheese salad (Nigel was also concerned that his Mark Two wife shouldn't let him down by becoming fat).

But she brought her meagre lunch through to the front room and while she watched an Australian soap opera—a minor enough vice but nonetheless one she would not have admitted to under torture—she kept glancing across towards "Acapulco." The removal lorry by now had gone, but there was still no sign of the owner's arrival.

When the moment did finally come, Vivvi nearly missed it. At a quarter past three she had had to leave for one

6

of the regular punctuations of her day, collecting her two children from school, and half an hour later, as she swung back into Smithy's Loam, she saw a large black limousine parked outside "Acapulco." Its uniformed driver, his beaming face reflecting the size of the tip he had received, was just getting into the car. He started the engine.

Vivvi slowed almost to a standstill, as if to give him room to pass, but since he was on the opposite side of the road, this was not a very convincing disguise for her curiosity.

"Why are we stopping, Mummy?" asked her six-year-old son from the back of the car.

"Just slowing down, Tom," Vivvi replied, peering at the doorway towards which the departing chauffeur waved. An ample white-haired woman was waving back. She must have been in her sixties, but was carefully and expensively preserved. Bright silk print dress, fur coat draped over shoulders, gleams of substantial jewellery, surprisingly high heels accentuating fine legs. There was about her a quality which, while not extreme enough to be dubbed "flashy" or "vulgar," would still have disqualified her from being called "self-effacing."

"Is that the lady who's going to live in Auntie Treezer's house?" asked Tom.

"Don't say *Auntie* Treezer." The reproof was automatic. Calling people who weren't relations "Auntie" was another usage Nigel had condemned as common.

Reluctantly, Vivvi swung the Peugeot 205 into the drive of "Haymakers." While she made much of letting Tom and his sister Emily out of the child-locked back, she could see the new resident still framed in her doorway, as if scenting the afternoon air.

The woman looked confident and peaceful, but alert. The feeling of slight uneasiness came back to Vivvi.

Tom and Emily had been given their tea and settled in front of children's programmes, which would keep them quiet until six o'clock. Vivvi hesitated by the window of her front room, about to close the curtains. It was nearly dark, seemingly darker than it had been only two days before when Theresa Cotton had come to say goodbye. But then of course it had been after six when Theresa Cotton had paid her visit.

Vivvi again looked down the close towards "Acapulco." Orangeish light spilled through the dimpled glass of the front door, but in the rest of the house the tightly drawn curtains gave no indication of which rooms were being used.

Vivvi felt she ought to do something, make some gesture, offer assistance to the new resident. But she wasn't sure what form her gesture should take. Her instinct was to go across and knock on the door, but she didn't think Nigel would approve of that. He frequently reverted to the point that people in the South don't wander in and out of each other's houses as much as in the North where Vivvi had been brought up.

So perhaps going across in person wouldn't be right. Anyway, she shouldn't really leave the children alone in the house, even just for a few minutes. One did hear of such terrible things happening.

No, maybe the answer was to do something more sedate. An official invitation. Yes, that would be more in keeping with Smithy's Loam.

Her mind made up, Vivvi drew the curtains and went to the telephone in the hall.

Some of the numbers were programmed into the memory and some weren't. In strict rotation she set the phone ringing in each of the other executive homes in Smithy's Loam. Number One ("High Bushes"), Number Two ("Perigord"), Number Four ("Hibiscus"), Number Five ("Cromarty"). In each case she invited the woman who answered to coffee on the Friday morning. All but one accepted.

Theresa's number was still on the memory. But of course it wasn't Theresa's number now. It belonged, together with the rest of "Acapulco," Smithy's Loam, to the new resident. The well-preserved lady who was providing so much new fuel for Vivvi's restless curiosity.

She punched up the number. It would be strange, she reflected, Smithy's Loam without Theresa . . . Well, she thought with a slight blush, without Theresa and Rod. But Rod had been away so much in recent months . . . And, anyway, Vivvi told herself, all the husbands remained shadowy figures in the life of Smithy's Loam.

The phone rang for a long time. She must be there. Vivvi was sure she would have noticed if the newcomer had left. Anyway, you wouldn't go out immediately after arriving in your new home, would you? Again, Vivvi felt that tweak of uncertainty, the fear that the new resident might not conform to accepted behaviour patterns.

What was her name? Theresa had said, Vivvi felt sure. An unusual name, she knew that much. But she couldn't for the life of her remember what.

At last the phone was answered, with a cheerful "Hello?"

"Oh, hello. My name's Vivvi Sprake. I live at Number Three, "Haymakers," up the top of the . . ." She just managed to stop herself saying "close." ". . . up at the top."

"Ah."

"I was really ringing just to welcome you to Smithy's Loam."

"That's very nice of you."

"I knew Theresa and Rod Cotton very well. I just wanted to say that I hope you'll be as happy here as they were."

"Thank you. Much appreciated."

"Actually, I was wondering if you'd like to come across for coffee one of these mornings, to meet a few of the other people in the . . ." Oh dear, she'd nearly said "close" again. Mustn't say "estate," either. And "development" sounded so bald and functional. "Um . . . in Smithy's Loam," Vivvi concluded.

"Yes, I'd enjoy that. Thank you."

"How about Friday?"

"Ah. Friday might be a bit difficult."

"Oh dear." Stupid. She should really have checked on the guest of honour's availability before setting up the others. It had just never occurred to her that someone moving to a new area might have other commitments.

"No, don't worry, Vivvi. I can juggle things round. Yes, Friday'd be fine. What sort of time?"

"Eleven?"

"Right. I'll look forward to meeting you then."

"And I'll look forward to meeting you. Oh, one thing . . ."

"Yes?"

"Sorry, I'm afraid I don't know your name."

"It's Pargeter."

"Mrs. Pargeter?"

"That's right. Mrs. Melita Pargeter."

CHAPTER THREE

Mrs. Pargeter slept well her first night in "Acapulco," Smithy's Loam. Better than she had expected to. First nights in strange rooms, she had found in the past, could prove restless and uncomfortable, so the deepness of her sleep seemed a good omen for her future in the new home.

The next day she was kept busy around the house, rearranging her furniture. She had some good pieces, and wanted to show them to their best advantage. The late Mr. Pargeter had left her well provided for in many ways, and each piece of furniture was like a little cassette of memory, which brought back vividly the circumstances of its purchase (or, when that was not the appropriate word, of its arrival in their marital home).

Some widows might have found these memories a cause

for tears, but all they prompted in Mrs. Pargeter was a grateful melancholy. She was not given to self-pity; when she looked back on her marriage, she did so with regret that it could not have continued longer, but also with appreciation of how good it had been while it lasted.

Much of the furniture had been in store for some time. Since her husband's death, Mrs. Pargeter had lived chiefly in hotels and rented accommodation. It had taken a few years until she felt ready to make another home, and "Acapulco," Smithy's Loam, was her first attempt in that direction.

She was still not certain that her choice of location had been right, but she was a philosophical woman, prepared to give the experiment six months and then, if it had not worked, concede failure and move on elsewhere. Thanks to the generosity and impeccably astute management of the late Mr. Pargeter, money was not a problem.

The house in Smithy's Loam had a lot going for it. Being of such recent construction, it was commendably easy to run. And the inevitable teething troubles of all new houses had been dealt with by the previous owners.

Also the development had the inestimable advantage for Mrs. Pargeter that its residents were not all elderly. Her experience of private hotels, like the Devereux in Littlehampton, had made her eager to avoid being compartmented into another geriatric ghetto. Though she had no illusions about the fact that she was in her late sixties, Mrs. Pargeter retained a lively interest in the world about her, and had come to the conclusion that this would be stimulated more by the company of younger people than by her contemporaries.

She had encountered so much distressing defeatism amongst the old, too many of whom seemed to regard their remaining years as a spiralling-down process. This was not Mrs. Pargeter's approach to any part of her life. Though she could not possibly know how many more years she would be allotted, she was determined to enjoy every one of them to the full.

She did not rush her furniture-shifting. Though in remarkably good condition for her age, Mrs. Pargeter recognised that now she had to husband her energy. So she worked in short bursts, with plenty of tea- and biscuit-filled intervals.

She had bought the Cottons' kitchen appliances, as well as their thick-pile carpets and Dralon curtains, all brand new a mere eighteen months before. Though they did not coincide exactly with her own taste, she could live with them. The time to make changes would be when her self-imposed six months' probation was over. If then she had decided that Smithy's Loam was for her, she would invest in decorations more expressive of her own personality. No point in splashing out all at once. In spite of her considerable wealth, Mrs. Pargeter was not careless with money. It was one of the many qualities in her which the late Mr. Pargeter had admired.

As she worked in the house that first day, and on her one necessary expedition down to the Shopping Parade (conveniently adjacent, a fact of which the original brochure for the development had made much), Mrs. Pargeter absorbed the atmosphere of Smithy's Loam. She was a woman of unusual perception and, though people were rarely aware of her scrutiny, little was missed by those mild blue eyes.

The main quality of the development which struck her was its neatness, its decorum, almost its formality. Though the houses were all of different designs and their plots of different shapes (indeed, that had been one of their chief selling points when first built), they had about them a uniformity.

Each lawn was punctiliously mowed and, though the clocks had already gone back to denote the end of Summer Time, the plants in the front gardens defiantly resisted the raggedness of autumn.

Each house was beautifully maintained. On each the paintwork and windows gleamed. So did the Volvos, Peugeots and Renault hatchbacks that stood in the drives, and so, when seen at the weekend, would the BMWs, Rovers and Mercedes that the husbands brought home.

The absence of men was another striking impression that Mrs. Pargeter received from Smithy's Loam. By the time she had woken on that first day, all of the husbands had left for work, and the early darkness ensured that the only evidence she would see of their homecomings would be the sweep of powerful headlights. All were of the aspirant classes; all worked long, ambitious hours to maintain the acquisitive executive standards of Smithy's Loam.

As a result of this, Mrs. Pargeter wondered whether she had moved into another kind of ghetto, a ghetto of women rather than of the old. Behind each immaculate, anonymous house front lay a female intelligence, with its own secrets, desires and ambitions. She was glad she had accepted the invitation for the Friday coffee morning. Already she was intrigued to meet the women, to find out how they spent their gender-segregated hours of daylight.

Darkness had fallen by half-past six when Mrs. Pargeter decided to call it a day. She was satisfied by what she had achieved. Already the careful disposition of her furniture had drawn attention away from the Cottons' carpets and curtains. Already the sitting-room at least bore a distinct Pargeter imprint. She felt she deserved a drink before she cooked her steak.

It was comforting to see bottles back in the glass-fronted corner cupboard which had been delivered to their Chigwell home one night at three a.m. after another of the late Mr. Pargeter's more spectacular business coups. She opened the doors, took out a glass and poured in generous measures of vodka and Campari. Then she went to the kitchen for ice and lemon.

It was there that she became aware of how cold the house had become. She went to the cupboard under the stairs, where the central heating controls were, to remedy the situation.

She switched the heating to "Constant." No indicator lights came on, but she gave the system the benefit of the doubt. It had worked perfectly to give her a hot bath that morning. She went into the sitting-room to enjoy her drink and wait for the house to warm up.

It didn't. After half an hour it was colder rather than hotter. She felt the largest radiator in the sitting-room. No heat at all.

She checked those in the hall. They were the same.

She opened the fusebox in the kitchen. But all the fuses were intact.

She looked again in the cupboard under the stairs. Still no indicator lights. More ominously, there was not even the softest hum from the boiler.

She paused for a moment in the hall. This was a nuisance. Of course she could ring up an emergency repair service. Or she could wait till the morning and summon someone less expensive to check the system out.

But, like anyone else in a new house, her first instinct was that she was at fault. She was unfamiliar with the controls and must have switched something off by mistake. If she did call a repair man, he would most probably walk straight in and, after the patronising flick of a single switch, overcharge grossly for her embarrassment and discomfiture.

It was probably something very simple. But, as the evening got chillier, Mrs. Pargeter wanted it sorted out. She hadn't paid all that money for a house to sit and freeze in it.

Of course the simplest thing would be to ring the former owner. Mrs. Pargeter didn't really want to do that on her first day of residence, but, on the other hand, Theresa Cotton had seemed an extremely amiable—if anonymous —young woman who, if it were a simple matter of one switch, would be only too ready to help out.

Mrs. Pargeter looked through her diary for the Cottons' new address. The husband, Rod, she recalled, had got some promotion which involved being based up North for a few years. Near York. Yes, that was right. Mrs. Pargeter found the address.

But there wasn't a phone number. Of course, she remembered now. Theresa Cotton had said the phone was only being connected the day they moved, and they hadn't yet been given the number.

Still, they'd been there nearly two days now. Mrs. Pargeter rang Directory Enquiries.

"What town, please?"

"It's near York. Place called Dunnington."

"And what name?"

"Cotton. The address is 'Elm Trees, Bascombe Lane.' "

There was a silence from the other end of the phone.

" 'Cotton' you said?"

"Yes."

"No. Sorry, no one of that name at the address you mention."

"They only moved in yesterday, and had the phone connected then."

"Just a minute. I'll check." Another silence. "No, no record of a new number for anyone by the name of Cotton. Sorry."

"Are you sure there isn't anywhere else you could check?"

"Certain, Madam. Maybe you were given the wrong address . . . ?"

"Hmm. Maybe. Thank you, anyway."

After she had put the phone down, Mrs. Pargeter looked thoughtful. She still looked thoughtful as she went through into the kitchen and started preparing her steak.

Must be Directory Enquiries' mistake—the service had gone downhill so much since privatisation, she decided, as she reconciled herself to a cold night. The paperwork on the Cottons' new number couldn't have got through. Or maybe there had been a delay on connecting the phone.

Yes, something like that.

It was odd, though . . .

CHAPTER FOUR

The next morning Mrs. Pargeter made no further attempt to contact Theresa Cotton. Instead, she risked the scorn of a gas repairman and was rewarded—or at least vindicated—by the discovery that there was something genuinely wrong with the central heating boiler.

The gas repairman, obedient to the long tradition of his calling, had not got the relevant replacement part with him, but managed, in direct contradiction to the long tradition of his calling, to locate and fit it within twenty-four hours.

So Mrs. Pargeter, with warmth now restored to her new home, thought no more about her failure to contact its former owner.

*   *   *

At eleven o'clock on the Friday morning there was more
concerted movement in Smithy's Loam than Mrs. Pargeter
had seen since her arrival.

Up until then she had noticed how rare it was to see
more than one of the residents walking out of doors at any
given time. Each morning, some time after the husbands
had left, there was a flurry of motorised departures, as those
women blessed with children took the second cars out for
the school runs. They did not all come back at the same
time, their returns staggered by the demands of shopping
and other errands.

Then, through the day, most of the residents would
make occasional forays on foot, to shop, to walk dogs, to
wheel infants. But these expeditions seemed rarely to coincide, and the Friday morning was the first occasion Mrs.
Pargeter had seen more than two of the women out at the
same time, as they converged on Vivvi Sprake's house.

She watched them through the net curtains left by the
Cottons. Mrs. Pargeter did not really like net curtains, but
the late Mr. Pargeter had always favoured them. Though
of course he never did anything in their marital home of
which he needed to be ashamed, he had always valued
privacy. One of his recurrent aphorisms had been, "What
is not seen requires no investigation." And his wife, re-
specting his judgement in all such matters, subordinated
her taste to his caution in the matter of net curtains.

She thought, as the newcomer, it would be appropriate
for her to arrive a little later than the others, and she
watched them as they crossed from their neat front doors
to Vivvi Sprake's equally neat front door. She had glimpsed
most of them during the preceding days and had already,

as most people do with unintroduced neighbours, formed impressions of them.

Vivvi was the only one she could actually identify by name, but the others she had christened in her own mental shorthand.

The six houses in Smithy's Loam curled in an elegant horseshoe around the road which enclosed the central green. Their individuality had been used as another selling point at the time of their building—look what an unregimented development this is, a random cluster of distinctively designed houses, all different, all set in plots of different shapes. But each plot had the same area and the conformity of materials used made the houses look more like a matching set than if they had been identical.

The resident of Number One, "High Bushes," directly opposite, had apparently not left the house since Mrs. Pargeter's arrival. But there was no doubt that she was there. Her windows also had the protection of net curtains, and from behind them a shadowy figure monitored each coming and going to the loop of road at whose entrance the house stood like a sentry-box. Each time Mrs. Pargeter entered her front door, she could feel the eyes boring into the back of her head, but whether their motive was malevolence or simple curiosity she could not tell.

In Mrs. Pargeter's mental shorthand, the woman in "High Bushes" became Mrs. Snoop the Spy.

She carried this Happy Families notation into her names for the other residents. Two women lived in Number Two, "Perigord." Mrs. Pargeter had in fact only seen one of them, but the existence of the other was a logical deduction. The one she had seen looked too young, and too uninterested in the pair of small children she shepherded, to be anything other than a foreign *au pair*. Mrs. Pargeter had dubbed her Miss Bored the Belgian's Daughter.

And in her fancy, Miss Bored's mistress, whose car left the close as early as those of the husbands, became Mrs. Busy the Businesswoman.

Vivvi Sprake's house was Number Three, incongruously called "Haymakers," and next door at Number Four, "Hibiscus," lived a woman whose hasty exits and averted eyes made her Mrs. Nervy the Neurotic.

Mrs. Pargeter's immediate neighbour at Number Five, "Cromarty," who had made no gesture of welcome to the newcomer but who cleaned her windows at least once a day, was dubbed Mrs. Huffy the Houseproud.

As she moved away from the net curtains and picked up her handbag, Mrs. Pargeter looked forward to putting real names to her cast of Happy Families' wives.

But of course at that stage she had no reason to suspect that amongst them might be included Mrs. Merciless the Murderess.

CHAPTER FIVE

Vivvi Sprake was an over-hearty presence in yellow dungarees, one of those people whose emotional range does not encompass subtlety.

"And what did your husband *do*, Mrs. Pargeter?"

The object of her interrogation gave an equable smile. "He was in business on his own account."

"Oh, what sort of line?"

"All kinds," Mrs. Pargeter replied, charmingly but uninformatively.

"Finance?"

"Yes."

"Commodities?"

"At times."

"Was he a broker?"

"That kind of thing, yes."

Vivvi seemed tacitly to recognise that that was as far as she was going to get, so she shifted her approach. "Carole's husband Gregory's in Commodities."

"Oh?"

"I assume you must have met Carole by now." Vivvi Sprake spoke with great care, restraining her northern accent as one might a kitten capable of suddenly breaking free to do something disgraceful on the floor. "I mean, with her being right next door to you."

"No, I haven't yet." So Mrs. Huffy the Houseproud was called Carole. Slowly the names were coming together.

"Oh well, I must introduce you." Vivvi darted away to collar a woman with rigidly coiffed blonde hair, who wore a grey blouse and matching skirt.

The quarry was brought forward for presentation to the guest of honour. "This is Melita Pargeter—Carole Temple."

"Hello." Carole made no pretence of being interested in her new neighbour.

"Hello, I've seen you cleaning your windows," said Mrs. Pargeter comfortably.

"Oh?" The tone implied affront.

"Well, I could hardly miss you, love, could I? I've been going in and out so much the last few days. You know how it is with a new house—you keep remembering things you've forgotten. Didn't you find that when you first moved in here?"

"No," Carole Temple replied. "But then my husband and I had made lists of all the things we might possibly need."

23

Yes, well, you *would* have done, wouldn't you, thought Mrs. Pargeter. She somehow couldn't see a close relationship developing with this neighbour.

Still, she went through the motions. "We're very conveniently situated here, though, aren't we? You know, for the shops. You can get virtually everything you need on the Parade, can't you?"

"Well, you *can*," Carole Temple conceded, "but they're all very over-priced. I go and do a weekly shop at Sainsbury's. And then once a month I stock up with basics at the Cash and Carry."

Once again, you *would*.

"I gather your husband's in Commodities," said Mrs. Pargeter, hoping that a change of subject might stimulate the conversational flow.

"Yes, he is," Carole Temple confirmed with a finality which confounded such hopes.

Mrs. Pargeter took refuge in a sip of coffee before attempting another foray. "Do you have children?" Surely that was a safe, uncontroversial subject.

"Two. At boarding school."

"Oh?"

Mrs. Pargeter waited for fond parental amplification of these minimal details, but she wasn't even granted the sex of the Temple offspring. All she got was: "Very expensive, boarding schools these days."

"So I believe."

"Do you have children?"

The suddenness of this enquiry took Mrs. Pargeter by surprise. But when she looked at Carole Temple's face she saw no flicker of interest; the question had been asked merely as a matter of convention.

"No. No, I don't." The fact was still a cause of mild

regret to her. But then, given the unpredictable demands made on the late Mr. Pargeter's time and his occasional absences, she had long ago concluded that their childlessness had probably been for the best. When they were together, they had been able to devote all their energies to each other.

By now roadblocks seemed to have been set up in all conversational avenues, and it was with some relief that Mrs. Pargeter saw Vivvi Sprake bearing towards her, bringing in her wake two women who, by a process of elimination, must be Mrs. Busy the Businesswoman and Mrs. Snoop the Spy.

CHAPTER SIX

~~~~~~

They were introduced to her respectively as Sue Curle and Fiona Burchfield-Brown. The former was in her early forties, a woman whose lined face enhanced rather than diminished her attractions. She had the rueful air of someone who has suffered but is not going to let that inhibit her future enjoyment of life.

But Fiona Burchfield-Brown, Mrs. Snoop the Spy, was the surprise. Mrs. Pargeter had been expecting someone beady and guarded, not the tall, slightly scruffy figure with the horse-brass scarf around her neck, who greeted her in exaggerated Sloane Ranger tones.

"Hello, such a pleasure to meet you." Mrs. Pargeter's hand was seized and clumsily shaken. There was about all of Fiona Burchfield-Brown's movements a coltish gaucheness, as if she had only just grown to her current dimensions and not yet learned to control her body.

"Sorry," she continued in her English public schoolgirl's voice, "I kept intending to come across and say hello, but I've had to wait in all week for these wretched little men who were supposed to be coming in to install the Jacuzzi. I didn't dare leave the house in case they arrived or rang up. My husband Alexander had set it all up and he'd have been frightfully cross if I'd missed them. Anyway, finally they ring this morning and say they're not coming till next week. Honestly. I ask you."

Well, at least that explained the apparent spying from behind the net curtains. Funny, though, thought Mrs. Pargeter, Fiona Burchfield-Brown didn't seem the sort to have a Jacuzzi. It was at odds with her slightly slapdash, eccentric aristocrat image.

As if anticipating this reaction, Fiona went on, "I don't really think we *need* a Jacuzzi. I mean, I can't see myself using it that much. Still, Alexander's very keen—lots of his chums in the City have got them—and he's the one who earns the money, so . . ." She shrugged helplessly.

"Weren't the Cottons planning to have one put in?" contributed Sue Curle.

"Well, it's certainly not there," said Mrs. Pargeter with a chuckle. "And I don't think I'm going to miss it either."

"No, no, I knew they hadn't had it done. It was only something they were planning. Rod was always talking about things he was going to do to the house—well, not *do*, but *have done*. And stuff they were going to buy . . . new video-camera . . . new compact disc player . . ."

"Oh, he was always on about that kind of thing," Fiona agreed.

"Yes, and I remember Theresa saying they were going

to have the kitchen done out," Sue Curle recalled. "And she was going to replace that dreadful old freezer."

"I don't remember Theresa having a freezer. Wasn't one in the kitchen, was there?"

"No, Fiona, she kept it in the garage. Great big antiquated lock-up one. Anyway, they were going to get a new one of those . . ."

"And they were even talking about buying a timeshare." Fiona Burchfield-Brown grimaced, perhaps at the vulgarity of the idea, and shrugged. "But then once his promotion came up, he rather lost interest in Smithy's Loam."

"That was when he was sent up North?"

"Yes, Mrs. Pargeter."

"Please call me Melita."

"Oh. Thank you." Mrs. Pargeter was by now accustomed to the slight hesitancy she heard in Fiona Burchfield-Brown's voice. Everyone seemed to have the same reaction to her name. Though granted the licence to use "Melita," few people took advantage of it. For most she seemed to remain "Mrs. Pargeter." And that state of affairs suited her well. Her Christian name retained its exclusivity, a bond between her and the late Mr. Pargeter.

"Did you know the Cottons well?" she hazarded.

Sue Curle shook her head. "Not really. Well, in the way you do know people with whom you have nothing in common but geography." Realising this might sound a little dismissive of present company, she covered it quickly. "I mean, obviously one does have friends locally, but the Cottons . . . well, we weren't particularly close. They were perfectly amiable . . . You know, we'd help each other out, water each other's plants when we went on holiday, that kind of thing . . . And, of course, one was always happy to, you know, pass the time of day . . ."

As these words were spoken, it struck Mrs. Pargeter how little "passing the time of day" she had so far witnessed in Smithy's Loam. The six houses seemed hermetically sealed units, their occupants completely self-sufficient. Oh yes, they'd come out for a social event like that morning's, but there was a kind of strain in the air. In spite of the proximity of the houses, nothing about Smithy's Loam gave any sense of community.

Of course, the atmosphere might be different at the weekends, when husbands and children were about, but somehow Mrs. Pargeter doubted it.

She turned to Fiona Burchfield-Brown. "Did you know them well?"

"The Cottons? No, not really. I mean, one made overtures. But Theresa tended to . . . well, keep herself to herself."

That tendency seemed to be an essential qualification for life in Smithy's Loam. In some ways, Mrs. Pargeter reflected, that would suit her well. Not in every way, though.

Sue Curle summed it up. "No, the Cottons were the standard issue Yuppie couple. Well, perhaps a bit too old to be proper Yuppies, but Rod had all the Yuppie values."

"Do you mean by that that Theresa didn't?"

"No. Not particularly. I assume she thought as he did. I don't know, she never talked about that kind of thing. As Fiona said, she kept herself to herself. At least, they never appeared to disagree. And they had no children to complicate things. Nice standard happily married little couple."

The bitterness in the voice prompted no more than a quizzical eyebrow from Mrs. Pargeter, but that was quite sufficient cue for Sue Curle. Like a scab waiting to be picked, the subject of her own marriage was not to be avoided.

"And no, in answer to your unspoken question, I am not part of such an ideal unit. I am in the throes of a particularly ugly divorce."

"I'm sorry."

"You don't have to be. At least not sorry for me emotionally. I'm delighted to get shot of the bastard. You can be sorry for me because the whole process takes so long and is so bloody exhausting, if you like."

Vivvi Sprake's doorbell rang and their hostess went off to answer it, as Fiona Burchfield-Brown leapt in to shift the conversation away from Sue's divorce. With a slight air of upper-class condescension, she said, "I think you'll find us a friendly enough lot around here, Mrs. Pargeter."

Mrs. Pargeter assessed the claim, and decided that so far the evidence did not support it.

"You know, I mean, we are all prepared to help each other out if something's important."

"Yes, like this new Indian restaurant proposal," said Sue Curle, pouncing on an object of dissatisfaction other than her husband. "Have you heard, Mrs. Pargeter, that coffee shop right on the corner of the Parade's for sale, and someone's applying for planning permission to turn it into an Indian restaurant?"

"No, I'm sorry. I'm still very new to the area."

"Well, I think we must all get together and see that it doesn't happen," said Sue Curle darkly.

"Yes," Fiona Burchfield-Brown agreed. "Alexander was going to write a letter to—"

"We needn't involve the bloody men!" Sue Curle snapped. "We women can set up our own protest group."

"Well, maybe . . ." Fiona, realising that the conversation was reverting to male shortcomings, turned again firmly to Mrs. Pargeter. "Anyway, as I say, if you've got any sort of problem, you can always ask any of us."

"Oh, thank you." But she thought she might be a bit careful which problems she did ask about.

The door from the hall opened, and Vivvi Sprake ushered in Miss Bored the Belgian's Daughter. The *au pair* was dressed in an expensive-looking leather jacket. Sue Curle looked up at her with annoyance.

"What is it?"

"I am sorry, Mrs. Curle," the girl replied, though there was no hint of apology in her tone. "They call from the office. Some crisis."

If part of the intention of the girl's stay in England was for her to learn the language, that part was not being fulfilled. Not a single vowel avoided mangling. And her accent suggested that Mrs. Pargeter's Happy Families shorthand had got the nationality wrong. The singsong intonation was not Belgian. More Scandinavian. Norwegian, perhaps . . . ?

"Oh, sod it. I told them I couldn't be in till this afternoon." But, even as she spoke, Sue Curle was picking up her handbag and rising to leave. "All right, Kirsten, you get back to the kids. You shouldn't have left them."

"But it was just for a few—"

"You shouldn't have left them," her employer repeated firmly.

Kirsten slunk sulkily from the room. Sue Curle said it had been a great pleasure to meet Mrs. Pargeter, that she looked forward to doing so again soon, and followed the *au pair* out.

Mrs. Pargeter saw them pass separately in front of Vivvi's picture window. On the other side of Smithy's Loam, Mrs.

Nervy the Neurotic had just come out of the drive of "Hibiscus." She made no gesture of acknowledgement to Sue or Kirsten, but walked briskly along, looking neither to right nor left.

She must have been invited, thought Mrs. Pargeter. And if she's only just going out now she must have been free to come. Or was there some feud amongst the residents of Smithy's Loam?

Vivvi Sprake, who had materialised beside her, followed Mrs. Pargeter's eyeline and confirmed her conjecture. "Jane Watson, that is. The missing guest. I did invite her. Said she couldn't come. Just that, didn't even bother to make up an excuse. Huh, stuck-up bitch."

And yet Mrs. Pargeter wondered if the description was fair. It was true, the way the woman strode ahead could look as if she was acting from arrogance. But the expression on her face belied that interpretation.

To Mrs. Pargeter's eyes, it looked more as if Jane Watson was motivated by fear.

CHAPTER SEVEN

Mrs. Pargeter put her feet up after lunch. It had been a tiring week. Not every day you move house. And, she thought as she looked fondly round the sitting-room she had now imprinted with her personality, I've achieved quite a lot. Certainly earned a little snooze in my own armchair.

The yielding upholstery and high back felt comfortingly familiar. After all the alien furniture of hotels and rented rooms, it was good to be among her own things.

The telephone woke her and for a second she wondered where she was. Then she reached for the receiver and read out the unfamiliar number.

"Could I speak to Mrs. Cotton, please?"

It was a man's voice. Oldish, sixties perhaps, and with

a slight fruitiness. The voice of a man used to speaking in public.

"I'm sorry. Mrs. Cotton has moved."

"Ah, she's actually gone, has she?"

"Yes," Mrs. Pargeter replied, slightly bewildered. "She moved out Monday evening."

"I know that was when she was intending to go, but I thought perhaps her plans might have changed."

"Not so far as I know."

"It's just, I was expecting to see her and . . . Look, never mind."

He sounded as if he was about to end the conversation, so Mrs. Pargeter interposed hastily, "I do have her new address, if that would help."

"Well, that wouldn't be any use to me, would it?" said the man rudely. "Goodbye." And he put the phone down.

Mrs. Pargeter was fully awake now. She stayed in her favourite armchair for a few moments, deep in thought. There was something odd. Why should the man have been so dismissive of the offered address? Was he only interested in Theresa Cotton while she lived in Smithy's Loam?

But no, that couldn't be it. He knew that she had been proposing to leave on the Monday evening. And he had implied that she had arranged to meet him and then not turned up.

The situation gave Mrs. Pargeter a strange but not wholly unfamiliar feeling, a compound of disquiet and of . . . yes, of excitement.

She picked up the telephone again and had another try at Directory Enquiries. Maybe the person she had spoken to on the Wednesday night had simply been inefficient. Maybe the paperwork of the Cottons' new telephone number had not percolated through the system.

Directory Enquiries answered. She gave exactly the same information as she had done on the previous occasion.

And got exactly the same reply. There was no one called Cotton with a telephone at the address she mentioned.

She stayed in her armchair for another moment's thought after she had put the phone down. Then she made up her mind and went into the hall to put on her fur coat.

The original brochure for Smithy's Loam did not mention, among its glowing list of the area's amenities, that the development was near to an excellent public library. But then that would not have been regarded as particularly important by the kind of people who were likely to buy that kind of property. When she had first visited "Acapulco" to inspect the property, Mrs. Pargeter had seen no evidence of any books anywhere.

To her, however, books were extremely important, and one of her first tasks on arrival had been to get herself issued with library tickets and stock up with her first week's reading.

But that afternoon her concern was with the reference section of the library, and this she found to be just as well stocked as the lending part. She explained the subject of her research to a most helpful librarian and was quickly directed towards the relevant maps, gazetteers and guide books.

It didn't take long to have her growing suspicion confirmed. She double-checked, cross-referencing different maps. Then checked again in a variety of indexes.

But the facts were incontrovertible. In the small town of Dunnington in North Yorkshire there was no road called Bascombe Lane.

And if the road didn't exist, then it couldn't contain a house called "Elm Trees."

In other words, Theresa Cotton had given a false address for her new home.

She had deliberately planned to go missing.

CHAPTER EIGHT

~~~~~~

Mrs. Pargeter called in at "High Bushes" on the way home. After she had rung the bell, she looked down the extremely sane paving to the wrought-iron gate set in a neat low wall. There was not a bush, high, low or of any other description, in sight. Either the original high bushes had since been cut down, or else the person who named the house had had a sense of humour.

Fiona Burchfield-Brown came to the door, and the look of surprise on her face suggested, as Mrs. Pargeter had suspected, that neighbourly calls were not common in Smithy's Loam.

Fiona, well-brought-up girl that she was, recovered quickly and invited her caller in.

"Well, just for a moment, thank you. It's getting chilly, these late afternoons, isn't it?"

Fiona Burchfield-Brown agreed that it was, as she ushered Mrs. Pargeter into the kitchen. Hoped she didn't mind it being the kitchen, but they were giving a dinner party that evening. No, Mrs. Pargeter didn't mind. She promised she wouldn't be long.

It's not fair to judge anyone on what their kitchen looks like when they're preparing a dinner party, but Fiona's did seem to be particularly untidy. The sink was piled high with crockery, and on every available surface utensils were spread about under a fine dusting of flour. In the middle of the floor a large, sloppy Labrador spread itself as only a Labrador can.

Fiona made the mandatory offer of tea or coffee, but was clearly relieved when Mrs. Pargeter, unwilling to compound the chaos, refused both. Returning to a slightly charred chicken carcase from which she proceeded inexpertly to remove the meat, Fiona asked what she could do to help her new neighbour.

Mrs. Pargeter had decided there was no need to share her suspicions. Remembering the late Mr. Pargeter's precept that one should always endeavour to tell the truth and nothing but the truth (though not necessarily the whole truth), she explained that she had had a phone call from someone asking exactly when Theresa Cotton had left Smithy's Loam. "And I didn't know *exactly*, Fiona, but I know you said you'd been watching out for your Jacuzzi people all week, so I thought you might have noticed."

Fiona Burchfield-Brown wrinkled her brow and then wiped it, leaving a little smear of chicken grease above her right eye. "Well, I think it was Monday evening. I'm sure it was. Theresa came round sort of sixish . . . to . . . well,

38

you know, to say goodbye, that sort of thing, and then, um, well, I saw the car drive off about . . . I don't know, seven, quarter past . . . But then it was back ten minutes later, and shortly after that, I suppose about half-past, it went off for good."

"And was Theresa alone when she left?"

"I don't think so. Well, put it this way, a man arrived shortly before she went and I didn't see him leave any other way, so I suppose he must have been in the car with her."

"Couldn't she have been driving him somewhere when she went off for the short trip at quarter past seven?"

"No. I think maybe he was driving the car that time. I'm not sure. It came out of the garage and drove off, then it came back ten minutes later, back into the garage, and the man came out of the garage and went to the front door again."

"And Theresa let him in?"

"I suppose so."

"So presumably she hadn't been in the car with him that time?"

"No, I suppose not."

"You didn't see him get in the car the second time?"

"No, but then I wouldn't have done. The car was in the garage, so they'd have gone through from the house to get into it."

"But didn't one of them get out of the car to close the garage door?"

Fiona stopped her dissection, Sabatier knife poised in midair. "Do you know, I don't think they did. That's strange, isn't it? I mean, when you're leaving somewhere for good, you'd surely make a point of locking up properly, wouldn't you?"

"Well . . ." Mrs. Pargeter shrugged casually. Then, unwilling to encourage thoughts of strangeness, she moved on quickly. "You didn't actually see that they were both in the car, did you?"

"No. I mean, it was after dark. I just saw the headlights go by. Couldn't really see inside. But they must have gone together, mustn't they?"

Not necessarily, thought Mrs. Pargeter, and then asked with an air of innocence, "The man wasn't Rod, was he?"

"Good Lord, no. I mean, I've hardly seen Rod since he got transferred up North, but he couldn't have changed that much. This man who came looked pretty scruffy. Wearing some sort of overall and a woolly hat, I seem to recall. And he had a beard. I mean, Rod would never have had a beard. He was a really fussy dresser, you know, the complete executive."

"Oh, well . . ." said Mrs. Pargeter, playing for time, wondering which tack to move on to next.

But fortunately Fiona, unprompted, filled the silence with more information. "I remember thinking at the time it was a coincidence Theresa should have two bearded men visit her the same day."

"Two . . . ?" Mrs. Pargeter echoed diffidently.

"Yes. The other one came early afternoon, while it was still light."

"You're sure it wasn't the same man?"

"Oh, quite sure. The afternoon one was much taller. And thinner. No, I could see him quite clearly."

"Did he arrive in a car?"

"No. Walked. He arrived about . . . half-past two, I suppose, rang the doorbell, Theresa let him in, and then he was there . . . I should think about half an hour."

"And was he smartly dressed?"

"No, he was scruffy, too. Really old clothes. You know, old to the point of being out of fashion."

"Ah." Mrs. Pargeter stood up. Didn't want to appear too inquisitive. "Well, look, thank you very much. If the gentleman rings back, I'll be able to give him chapter and verse of Theresa Cotton's departure."

"Yes." Fiona started to rub her greasy hands on an equally greasy tea towel. "Let me—"

"Please, don't worry. I'll see myself out."

"Oh, well, if you're sure. I am a bit up to my ears . . ." Fiona looked around the kitchen in a kind of despair tinged with panic. How on earth would she ever get a Cordon Bleu meal together and get the place tidied up and change before her guests arrived?

"Oh, one thing . . ." Mrs. Pargeter hovered in the doorway. "The man who rang also asked for Theresa's new address. And I couldn't find the piece of paper that I'd scribbled it down on. I don't suppose, by any chance . . . ?"

"Yes, she did give it to me. Let me think. I remember, I asked for it just as she was leaving. And she told me and I scribbled it on the pad on the telephone. It's in the hall. You'll see it as you go out."

"Oh, thank you so much." Again Mrs. Pargeter turned to go, and again stopped. "I'm sorry, there's one other thing, Fiona. This really is the last one, I promise. Then I'll leave you to get on with things."

"No problem," said Fiona. No, Mrs. Pargeter's questions weren't a problem; compared to the problem of getting this dinner party together, everything else paled into insignificance.

"I just wondered if you knew the name of the removal

41

firm that Theresa used. I've a feeling they may have taken some light fittings that were meant to be left, and I want to check with them."

Well, it was only a small lie. The late Mr. Pargeter wouldn't have minded that. He had always been a pragmatist; he didn't object to lies on principle, only when they were likely to lead to further lies and complications of consistency.

"Yes, I remember," said Fiona helpfully. "Couldn't forget it, really, seeing that dirty great lorry opposite for the best part of a day. They were called Littlehaven's."

"Ah."

"I remember thinking it was an unusual name. Didn't recognise it. Certainly not one of the local firms. But I suppose she wouldn't necessarily use a firm from down here if she was moving up North."

No, she wouldn't, thought Mrs. Pargeter. Not if she *was* moving up North.

The hall was dominated by a large coatstand with a mirror, from whose hooks an assembly of Barbour coats, tweed caps and green quilted jerkins hung. In the umbrella-rack at the bottom stood a shooting-stick, a few golf clubs and a riding crop. As Fiona had promised, there was a pad of paper on a low table by the telephone. Mrs. Pargeter had to turn back several pages before she came to the scrawled address.

"Elm Trees, Bascombe Lane, Dunnington, North Yorkshire."

At least Theresa Cotton's lies had been consistent.

CHAPTER NINE

It was after half-past five when Mrs. Pargeter crossed from the misnamed "High Bushes" to "Acapulco" and, since the next stage of her investigation required another trip to the library, there was nothing more she could do that day. So she happily resigned herself to a nice dinner and an early night.

The nice dinner was poached salmon trout, followed by profiteroles. After her peregrinations of the last few years, Mrs. Pargeter found it a great pleasure to have her own kitchen to cook in again. She had never had inhibitions about preparing full meals when she was on her own; she did not subscribe to the boiled egg and cottage cheese conspiracy. The late Mr. Pargeter, the nature of whose work sometimes prevented him from being with her in the evenings, had always encouraged her to eat properly.

With the meal she drank a rather good bottle of Sancerre. That was another pleasure of the new house, having a permanent home for the excellent cellar the late Mr. Pargeter had assembled.

When she had tidied up the meal, Mrs. Pargeter drank a little Armagnac and retired early to bed to sleep the dreamless sleep of the innocent.

The same helpful librarian directed her next morning to the complete set of Yellow Pages and, after consulting the "Removals and Storage" section of some dozen volumes, Mrs. Pargeter found the name she was looking for.

Littlehaven's were based near Worcester. Certainly a long way from the Surrey of Smithy's Loam. And not a logical step in the direction of Dunnington in North Yorkshire, even if that address had not already been discredited.

Mrs. Pargeter took down the address and phone number of the firm, and walked back to her new home.

There was more activity on the Shopping Parade on a Saturday morning than during the week. Volvo, Peugeot and Mercedes estates were backed up to the shops, the great maws of their hatchbacks gaping to consume the cartons of food, the cases of wine, the boxes of electronic gadgetry, the pots of paint, the ready-to-assemble furniture and all the other credit-card booty of their owners. Whatever troubles the area might have, lack of money (or at least lack of credit) was not among them.

At the end of the Parade, Mrs. Pargeter noted, with a wry smile, the run-down coffee shop, which was under threat of translation into an Indian restaurant. From Mrs. Pargeter's point of view the proposed change seemed an excellent idea. Nothing she liked better than a good hot curry, and to have a takeaway within fifty yards of her house sounded an ideal arrangement. Her fellow-residents, though, she had gathered, might not share that view.

In Smithy's Loam the husbands' cars glistened outside the houses. A moustached man who was presumably Carole Temple's husband Gregory, the commodity broker, was outside "Cromarty" in a designer tracksuit cleaning his BMW. He gave no acknowledgement to Mrs. Pargeter as she walked up her garden path. And when, a few minutes later, a grey-haired man who must have been Nigel Sprake emerged from "Haymakers" and slùng a golf bag into the back of his Renault 25, Mr. Temple gave him no more than a cursory nod.

The realisation came to Mrs. Pargeter of how safe Theresa Cotton had been when she gave her neighbours a false address. However much the residents of Smithy's Loam might gush over each other at a coffee morning, there was no real contact there. Someone who left the area was instantly blanked out from the screens of the others' selfishness. There was no danger of any of them ever trying to make contact with Theresa again.

Without much expectation of success, Mrs. Pargeter punched up the Littlehaven's number. There was no one in the office over the weekend, but if she cared to leave a message on the ansaphone . . . She didn't bother. What she wanted to find out would require a more delicate approach than a recorded message.

Never mind, she would continue her enquiries on the Monday.

She pottered around the house for the rest of the morning, and prepared herself a herb omelette for lunch. On the occasions when she looked through her net curtains,

Smithy's Loam proved, in accordance with her expectations, to be as quiet at weekends as it was during the week. A few of the cars left and returned with full family loads, but for most of the morning the loop of road and pavement remained empty. The children, if out of doors, would be playing in their back gardens; no one would be so "common" as to allow them to play in the street. Anyway, wouldn't it be dreadful if childish feet scarred the baize-like smoothness of the green central reservation?

Mrs. Pargeter was glad she had planned a treat for herself that weekend. It had been a hard week. She deserved a little pampering.

Promptly at three o'clock, the limousine arrived for her. By then she was dressed in another of her bright silk print dresses and wearing a considerable array of jewellery. The mink coat draped over her shoulders was longer than the one she had been wearing on the day of her arrival. An exotic evening dress was packed in the neat overnight case the chauffeur carried down to the limousine.

Just as she was getting into the car, the sour commodity broker emerged from the front door of "Cromarty," carrying electric hedge clippers with which to scrape another unnecessary millimetre off his perfect front hedge. Mrs. Pargeter was gratified to see that he gave her an involuntary look of impressed surprise.

On the way up to London she chattered amiably to the chauffeur, asking tenderly after his geographically extended family. She always used the same man, whose name was Gary. He had been employed on numerous occasions by the late Mr. Pargeter, but after his patron's death had adapted to a slower style of driving. When he started his own business, he had offered to ferry Mrs. Pargeter wherever she wished to go free of charge, in recognition of all that her husband had done for his career, but she always insisted on paying him. Like her late husband, Mrs. Pargeter was a great believer in the encouragement of free enterprise.

The chauffeur delivered her to the Savoy, where she checked into her room and changed into a beautifully cut rich lilac evening dress. She dined early in the hotel, and went by taxi to see a new musical which had received extravagantly favourable notices. Back at the hotel she had half a bottle of champagne in her room.

She woke too late the next morning to bother about breakfast, but made up for it with a huge traditional English lunch.

On the dot of three-thirty the limousine arrived to take her back to Smithy's Loam.

It had been a very restful weekend. Among the many things for which she had to be grateful to the late Mr. Pargeter was the way he had taught her to enjoy treats.

CHAPTER TEN

Mrs. Pargeter began the continuation of her campaign at nine-thirty sharp on the Monday morning. She got through to Littlehaven's straight away.

"Oh, good morning. My name is Pargeter. I wonder if you could help me? I'm ringing about a removal job you did last week."

"Listen," a truculent male voice objected, "if you've got any complaints, you should've got back to us within twenty-four hours. We can't possibly be expected to—"

"It isn't a complaint."

"Oh," said the voice, partly mollified but still wary.

"You see, I'm the person who's moved into the house from which you removed the previous owner's possessions."

"If anything got left behind, we must've had instructions about it. My men are very thorough. They don't go around—"

"No, no, it's all right." Mrs. Pargeter was beginning to wonder whether paranoia was an occupational hazard of furniture removers. "The fact is," she continued, "that the former owner of the house did give me her address, but I've lost the piece of paper she wrote it on and I am sure you must have on your records some—"

"Look, if you want a flaming Missing Persons bureau," the voice complained, unaware of how apt its words were, "you've come to the wrong place. I'm running a removals business here. I haven't got time to bust a gut chasing information about—"

It wasn't worth pointing out that in the time he had taken to say all that, he could have found the information and given it to her. Instead, soothingly, she interrupted, "That wasn't the only reason for my call. I might also be putting some business your way."

The lie had the required effect. "Oh. What sort of business?"

"Um . . . A removal job," she replied, thrown by the question.

"Well. In that case . . . who was the person you were enquiring about . . . you know, last week's job . . . ?"

"The name was Cotton. Smithy's Loam."

"Oh, yes. The Surrey job. Long way for us, that is. Don't usually go that far. So what was it you wanted to know?"

"The Cottons' new address. Where you delivered to the other end."

The voice laughed harshly. "Well, we didn't deliver the other end, did we?"

49

"What, you mean you got there and found the address didn't exist?" Her question burst out instinctively.

"Eh?" The voice sounded bewildered. "No, of course we didn't. It wasn't a removal job from one house to another. It was a storage job."

"So you mean you now have all the Cottons' furniture in store?"

"That's right. In containers. In our warehouse. Five miles away from here."

"Ah." The extent of the planning behind Theresa Cotton's disappearance was becoming clearer by the minute. "And did Mrs. Cotton say how long she wanted everything stored?"

"Well, she paid for six months in advance. Said it might be longer, though. Her husband had got some posting abroad or something."

"Really?"

"Look, what is this?" The voice was again becoming suspicious. "Why are you asking all this stuff?"

"Well, as I say, what I really wanted was the Cottons' new address . . ."

"I haven't got it. And if you don't mind, I—"

"But, in fact," Mrs. Pargeter came in quickly, "I was asking because it's a storage job that *I* need doing."

"Oh." Once again the voice was calmed by an appeal to the profit motive. "What is it? Full house contents?"

"Yes."

"Well, as I say, we do containerised storage . . ."

"Yes, but you can store everything, can you? I mean, furniture, domestic appliances . . . ?"

"The lot. Nothing perishable, of course, but everything else."

"And everything would be safe in your warehouse? I mean, from burglars and—"

"Safe as houses, lady." The voice allowed itself a brief joke. "Safer than most houses, actually."

"Oh, that's most interesting. Could you tell me how much that would cost?"

The voice reeled off a list of figures, with variations for the volume of goods stored and the period of storage. It concluded, "Let me take your particulars and then I can send you details through the post."

"Yes. Thank you. Of course I am just getting quotes at the moment."

"Shopping around, you mean?"

"Yes."

"Right." The voice turned shirty. "Look, you've wasted quite enough of my time this morning. When you've got a serious business proposition, ring back. Otherwise don't bother!"

This time Mrs. Pargeter was not quick enough to stop the voice from putting the phone down. Though she wasn't sure what she could have said, anyway.

Oh, well, she'd got some useful information. Pity she hadn't been able to get more. Littlehaven's must have had some contact address for the Cottons. Surely they wouldn't do business with people of no fixed abode . . . ?

On the other hand, they had been paid for six months in advance. And, in a sense, the storage company had the advantage. The complete contents of a house were worth quite a bit of money. They wouldn't anticipate anyone just leaving the stuff in their custody without reclaiming it. No, the goods were there as hostages against default of payment.

Anyway, given the thoroughness with which Theresa Cotton had disseminated her other lies, Mrs. Pargeter felt sure she could have come up with something to cover this eventuality. The lie about not having the phone connected until they moved in had been glib enough; Theresa could easily have fabricated something else . . . Her husband was being posted abroad, but they didn't know exactly where they'd be living yet . . . ? They'd get in touch as soon as they had a permanent address . . . ? Yes, that'd be good enough to satisfy the voice on the phone. Particularly if he'd got six months' advance payment in his pocket.

For a moment Mrs. Pargeter wondered whether the story about a foreign posting for Rod Cotton could be true . . .

But no, surely not. If that were the case, then Theresa could have told everyone. In fact, given the emphasis in Smithy's Loam on success and promotion, she would definitely have told everyone. She wouldn't go to the trouble of inventing false addresses in North Yorkshire.

Unless, of course, the foreign posting was a demotion. Things hadn't worked out for Rod in the North and now he had been forced to go abroad to get a job which would keep up their living standards . . . ?

But somehow that didn't seem very convincing, either.

Basically, Mrs. Pargeter told herself, this is all conjecture. I don't have enough facts yet.

Still, she hadn't come to the end of her resources. There remained a variety of ways of getting more facts.

"Oh, hello, Vivvi. This is Melita Pargeter."

"How nice to hear you. I hope you had a good weekend."

"Delightful, thank you."

"Yes, not a lot happens round the close"—damn, she'd let it slip out—"at weekends, but I think that's just the time when you can appreciate how secluded we are here. You really could be in the middle of the country at the weekends. Didn't you find that?"

"I'm afraid I can't say. I was up in London."

"Oh." This again felt wrong to Vivvi. People who had just moved to Smithy's Loam should stay in Smithy's Loam. They shouldn't go gallivanting up to London at the first opportunity.

"Anyway, Vivvi, I was just ringing to thank you so much for Friday."

"Oh, it was a pleasure."

"No, most kind of you to set it up. I was delighted to have the opportunity to meet everyone."

"Well, we are all so glad you could come." But somehow the use of the word "we" seemed inappropriate in Smithy's Loam.

"I'd love to repay the compliment at some point."

"Oh, that'd be terrific. I'd love to come, but, you know, I do get very tied up with the kids and . . ."

"Yes. Yes, well, we'll sort out a time." But as she said the words, Mrs. Pargeter felt no urgency to leap for her calendar.

"Oh, incidentally, Mrs. Pargeter, did you hear that Sue Curle is trying to set up a women's action group to stop this Indian restaurant menace . . . ?"

"She mentioned something about it. I didn't realise she'd actually set up a group."

"Well, she's setting it up. I do hope we can count on your support."

Not, Mrs. Pargeter decided, the moment to say what an enormous convenience she thought a nearby Indian restaurant would be. No need to ruffle the neighbourhood feathers yet. "Oh, I'd certainly be interested to hear more about it," she said prudently. "Was Theresa Cotton against it?"

"What?"

"This Indian restaurant. Did she oppose the idea?"

"Um . . ." Vivvi Sprake sounded as if she was racking her brains to recall who Theresa Cotton was. "Oh, I don't think we'd heard about the planning application before she left."

"It was only a week ago."

"Was it really? It seems ages."

"Did you see her before she left?"

"Theresa? Yes, she did just drop round to, you know, say goodbye before she was off."

"On the Monday evening?"

"Yes."

"Ah."

"Anyway," said Vivvi forcibly, "thank you so much for calling, Mrs. Pargeter. I do appreciate it."

"Oh, one thing, Vivvi . . ."

"Yes?"

"I've actually been trying to contact Theresa Cotton, but I haven't managed to get through." That at least was absolutely true. "Just something I need to check on the house. I wondered if you could tell me who Rod Cotton works for . . . ? I thought I could try and contact him instead."

"Yes, of course. He's with C, Q, F & S. Just a min, I've got the number here in my address book." She gave it. "I mean, that's the number of the main office down here." A slight unidentifiable change seemed to have come into Vivvi Sprake's voice. "I haven't got the number of the Yorkshire branch. But the main office'd be able to tell you."

"Yes. Yes, of course. Well, that's very kind of you, Vivvi. And once again, thank you so much for Friday."

As she put the phone down, Mrs. Pargeter looked puzzled.

What was the strange note that had come into Vivvi Sprake's voice when she started talking about Rod Cotton? And, come to that, why had Vivvi Sprake got Rod Cotton's old office number in her address book?

CHAPTER ELEVEN

One of the luxuries of Mrs. Pargeter's new home was its plethora of telephones. There was one in the sitting-room, one in the main bedroom and one in the hall. It was the last of these that she had used to phone Littlehaven's. Somehow being in the hall seemed more purposeful, more businesslike than operating from the comfort of her favourite high-backed armchair.

The hall phone stood on a little shelf just above a central heating radiator. Deciding it was still a little early to put her call through to "C, Q, F & S" (whatever they might be), she turned away towards the kitchen to make herself a cogitative cup of coffee. But, in doing so, she dislodged the scrap of paper on which she had written the firm's number and watched with dismay as it slipped against the wall and disappeared down the back of the radiator.

One of the annoying things about moving into a new house is that, though you quickly know where the large items in your possession are, it takes some time before you locate all the small but crucial pieces of impedimenta that make life possible. Amongst such pieces of impedimenta that Mrs. Pargeter could not at that moment find was something long enough to reach behind the radiator and retrieve the missing telephone number.

It was ridiculous. There must be something in the house, she told herself. She went through the kitchen and tried the handles of various brooms and sweepers, but they all proved too thick to fit the narrow space. She went out to the shed, but encountered the same problem with all of her garden tools. She tried upstairs, rifling through cupboards and some still unpacked boxes in one of the spare rooms, but again drew a blank.

This was infuriating. She must have *something*. It would be too pathetic to have to knock on one of the other front doors of Smithy's Loam to ask for help.

She stood on the landing in a quandary of irritation. It was such a simple thing she was looking for. Mrs. Pargeter prided herself on her independence, and was determined not to be defeated by something so trivial.

It was then that she remembered the late Mr. Pargeter's swordstick.

She had put it in one of her high bedroom cupboards the previous week, and now she had to climb on a chair to get it down.

The stick felt reassuringly smooth and solid in her hand. Its dark wood tapered down to a brass ferrule and was topped by a substantial brass grip in the shape of some fanciful heraldic beast. Remembering its secret, Mrs. Pargeter gave the grip two little half-twists and withdrew the gleaming blade. It was nearly three feet long and at no point wider than an inch. Both edges and the point were razor-sharp.

The late Mr. Pargeter had abhorred violence, and it was his proud boast that he had never had occasion actually to use the swordstick. However, there had been occasions in his particular line of business when he had found its presence in his hand a considerable source of reassurance.

As she went downstairs, Mrs. Pargeter looked at her watch and saw with irritation that it was now half-past ten. Her search of the house had taken a disproportionately long time. Still, at least it was no longer too early to make the call which she hoped would locate Rod Cotton.

She squinted down behind the radiator and saw how the paper was trapped. It was caught on the ledge at the top of the skirting-board. She slid the swordstick blade down the gap from above and worked it along to dislodge the missing phone number.

Successful first time. The sheet of paper fluttered on to the carpet at her feet.

But that was not the only object which the swordstick dislodged.

There was also a letter with a first-class stamp but no postmark. It was addressed in a firm feminine hand to: "Brother Michael, The Church of Utter Simplicity, Dunstridge Manor, Dunstridge, Sussex."

The decision to open the letter was made instantly. Though Mrs. Pargeter had a proper respect for individual privacy, she felt that Theresa Cotton's subterfuge with the false address justified a relaxation of customary moral usages. And she knew that the letter had been written by the former occupant of "Acapulco." They had had correspondence about the details of the fittings which were to be left in the house, and Mrs. Pargeter recognised the handwriting.

The letter must have slipped off the telephone shelf, just as the piece of paper had, and, probably in the confusion of moving, Theresa Cotton had forgotten that it had never reached the post-box.

Mrs. Pargeter opened the letter and read it, still standing in the hall.

It was written on notepaper headed with the Smithy's Loam address and dated the Thursday before the move.

Dear Brother Michael,

Most of my preparations are now made and I cannot wait to get this part of my life over with. Ever since I made the most important decision of my life, time has dragged painfully.

I have thought over what you said about the money at our last meeting, and have decided that I would rather hand over the cheque at my Becoming Ceremony. Somehow that seems right to me. At the moment that I shed the personality of Theresa Cotton and become Sister Camilla, I want also to shed the material trappings of Theresa Cotton. I hope you understand. Apart from anything else, the money will not be through until the house sale actually takes place, and I don't like the idea of writing postdated cheques.

I have also given a lot of thought to what you said about my mental preparation, particularly about getting my mind into a state of maximum receptiveness. I know that I should clear it of all grudges and resentment, as well as of material thoughts. I must confess at the moment I am finding getting rid of the material thoughts easier than the others! But I will keep trying. I think the solution will probably be for me to wait until I am about to leave and then, in as short a time as possible, to go and see all the people towards whom I feel resentment or about whom I know secrets, and just talk to them, clear the air. As you said, confrontation of the things that worry us is always better than avoidance. Otherwise bad thoughts grow and fester. I am determined to come to you with a mind as free of the past as I can make it. With a mind in which there is as much room as possible for God.

Following your advice, I have worked out a way of obscuring my precise destination when I leave here. I am sure God will forgive me a small lie in such a good cause! So far my story has not raised any awkward questions and, given the lack of interest in others amongst most of the people of my acquaintance, I don't see why it ever should!

As I said when we last spoke, I propose to leave here on Monday evening, but I do not wish to come straight to the Church. Some instinct tells me that I will need twenty-four hours' break between my old life and the new. I will come to the Church next Wednesday in the morning, with my mind clear and unsullied by material or evil thoughts. The time cannot come too quickly when I will be with you in God.

Yours ever (though not much longer, thank God, in this identity)

Theresa Cotton

Well, thought Mrs. Pargeter, there's a turn-up.

CHAPTER TWELVE

~~~~~~~~~~~~~~~~~~~~~~~~~~~~~~~~~~

On the other hand, it did make a lot of things clear. If Theresa Cotton was about to enter some sort of religious order and make a complete break from the galloping consumerism of her old life, at least some of her behaviour was explained.

But the explanation only went so far. And in fact it raised almost as many questions as it answered. Particularly, it raised questions about her husband. Was Rod Cotton aware of his wife's plans, was the change in her lifestyle something which they had discussed? Or had he, like everyone else, been misled by false information? Was Theresa intending just to vanish from his life and spend the rest of her days as Sister Camilla? Come to that, did Rod know that his wife proposed to donate the proceeds of their house sale to some obscure religious foundation?

What on earth *was* the Church of Utter Simplicity? Mrs. Pargeter felt certain that she had never heard the name before. There were some alternative sects which were never out of the news, usually with bad publicity, but this one was completely unfamiliar. What were the precepts of the Church of Utter Simplicity? And how much money were they hoping to receive from their latest convert?

Mrs. Pargeter hesitated for a moment. Now, thanks to the letter, even though it did raise all these questions, she knew where Theresa Cotton had gone. Though she might not approve of the deception the woman had practised, the mystery was cleared up. The more dramatic explanations of Theresa Cotton's disappearance which had been encroaching on Mrs. Pargeter's thoughts could be dismissed. The truth was bizarre, but at least it did explain things. The fortunes of the Cottons were now no longer Mrs. Pargeter's business.

And yet . . .

There was still something that niggled in her mind. To call it an anxiety would have been to overstate the case, but there was a little shadow of disquiet there. Something didn't quite add up, and Mrs. Pargeter knew that she wouldn't really relax until she had checked just one or two details.

All she needed to do was confirm the truth of what the letter implied, and then her mind would be set at rest.

Though the existence of the Church of Utter Simplicity sounded much less likely than that of "Elm Trees," Bascombe Lane, Dunnington, Directory Enquiries had no difficulty in providing her with its number.

She rang through and was quickly answered by an efficient American female voice. "Church of Utter Simplicity."

The words still sounded incongruous to Mrs. Pargeter, but she supposed that if you said them every time the phone rang they ceased to be odd. Certainly the American voice gave no sign of being amused.

"Good morning. Could I speak to Brother Michael, please?"

"Just a moment."

The line clicked, then she heard, "Hello? Brother Michael speaking."

The fruitiness of the voice was unmistakable. It was the man who had interrupted her sleep on the previous Friday afternoon, the man who had asked her where Theresa Cotton was. Just as she was now asking him. The little flicker of disquiet in Mrs. Pargeter's mind pulsed more strongly.

"Good morning," she said without identifying herself. "I am trying to contact a Mrs. Theresa Cotton . . ."

"Oh," said the man's voice. "I didn't know anyone knew she was supposed to be coming here."

"She did confide in a few friends," Mrs. Pargeter lied.

"That was foolish of her." As in their previous conversation, the man made no attempt to be pleasant.

"Well, since I do know she's there," Mrs. Pargeter insisted, "I wonder if it would be possible for me to speak to her . . . ?" Though quite what she'd say if her request was granted Mrs. Pargeter had no idea.

This was a problem she did not have to face, because Brother Michael immediately snapped, "No. If she were here, you wouldn't be allowed to speak to her, anyway. That is not the sort of contact we encourage for our members. But, since she isn't here—"

"She *isn't* there? But she told me that she was going to join you last Wednesday."

"That is what she told me," said Brother Michael in an aggrieved tone. "However, she didn't appear last Wednesday."

"Oh?"

"And she hasn't appeared since. But, if you do see her," he continued, anger building in his voice, "please tell her that her change of mind—if that's what it is—has caused great inconvenience to me, and wouldn't, I'd have thought, have done her much good with the Living God! Goodbye!"

And the phone was slammed down.

The disquiet in Mrs. Pargeter's mind by now would have qualified for the description of anxiety.

"Hello? C, Q, F & S."

If Mrs. Pargeter had been hoping that the girl on the switchboard might give some helpful gloss on what those initials stood for, she was destined to be disappointed.

"Oh, good morning. Could I speak to Mr. Rodney Cotton, please?"

There was a silence from the other end. Then, presumably having checked in some list, the girl announced, "Sorry, we don't have anyone of that name working here."

"Ah," said Mrs. Pargeter, sticking to her prepared script. "It's possible that he may have been transferred to your northern branch. Could you give me their number?"

"Do you mean Carlisle, York or Blackburn?"

"York."

The girl gave the number. Mrs. Pargeter rang through to York and received exactly the same answer as she had in London. The accent was different, but the message was the same. "Sorry, we don't have anyone of that name working here."

She thought about it. Southerners are extraordinarily vague about the North of England; for most of them Carlisle, York or Blackburn would be pretty much interchangeable. To the denizens of Smithy's Loam Rod Cotton would just have gone "up North." Perhaps it was only the false address Theresa had given that had pinpointed York.

Mrs. Pargeter went back to Directory Enquiries and got the Carlisle and Blackburn numbers of C, Q, F & S. She also got some extra information gratis when the man said, "Oh, you mean the computer people?" So at least she now knew in which industry Rod Cotton worked.

Carlisle hadn't heard of him.

Nor had Blackburn.

Puzzled and by now quite uneasy, Mrs. Pargeter again rang the London number and asked to be put through to the Personnel Department.

"Good morning," she said to the fast-talking young man who answered. "I'm trying to make contact with one of your employees."

"Oh yes?"

"A Mr. Rodney Cotton."

"Just a moment." There was a silence. No rustling of papers, so presumably he was checking some computer record. "No. Sorry. No one of that name."

"Well, that's most odd. I mean, I know he was definitely working in your London branch six months ago."

"Six months ago? Just a moment." Another silence, while further data was summoned up on to a screen. "Oh yes. Rodney Cotton. Yes, he was one of our Sales Directors. He doesn't work here any longer."

"What?"

"The company let him go."

"Let him go?"

"Took him out."

"Took him out?"

"Yes, took him out! Oh, for heaven's sake, don't you understand—he was fired."

"Fired?" Mrs. Pargeter echoed softly.

"Yes. You understand that word, don't you?"

"Yes. Yes, I do. So what you're saying is that Rodney Cotton hasn't worked for your company for the last six months?"

"Exactly."

"And you're sure he wasn't transferred to one of your northern branches?"

"Madam, he has not worked for any part of C, Q, F & S since the eleventh of March this year."

"Oh. What, so, I mean, would he have got some sort of redundancy payment?"

"I daresay he'd have got some sort of package, but not a great deal. He hadn't been with us that long. He went as part of the rationalisation earlier this year."

"Oh. I don't suppose, by any chance," Mrs. Pargeter asked politely, "you would know where he's working now . . . ?"

There was a grim laugh from the young man in Personnel. "I'm sorry. I don't know. Mind you, I think he'd be lucky to be working anywhere."

"What do you mean? Was he very bad at the job?"

"I've no idea. Never met the poor devil. All I mean is his end of the business is not exactly a growth area at the moment. There was a lot of over-recruitment in sales when micros were first launched. Now the balance of the market's shifted, I'm afraid there are a good few people like Mr. Cotton around."

"And all chasing the same few jobs?"

"That's it. What I'm saying, Madam, is if Mr. Cotton has now got another job at the same sort of level as he had here, then he's performed a bloody miracle."

Mrs. Pargeter thanked the young man for his help and went into the kitchen finally to make herself that cup of coffee. She needed it.

Nestled into her favourite armchair, she took a welcome sip and gave in to the stampede of thoughts rampaging through her head.

Now there was not just one missing person who had covered their tracks with lies. There were two.

And one of them might have been missing for as long as six months.

CHAPTER THIRTEEN

It was time, Mrs. Pargeter decided, to summon help. She was fortunate in having a rich repertory of assistants on whose services she could call. Their names were contained in the late Mr. Pargeter's address book, which, she sometimes considered, was the most valuable part of the rich estate he had left her. It was an unrivalled list of contacts which, had it fallen into the wrong hands, could have caused considerable unpleasantness.

Mrs. Pargeter looked up the name "Wilson" and dialled the number listed there. The gentleman who replied identified himself as "Mickey's Motors" and regretted that Mr. Wilson no longer worked with him. "No, he's gone up in the world. West End, now. Big showroom in Hanover Square. Only deals in Rollers and Bentleys, that kind of stuff. Mind you, sure I can help. Got a great little 'B'-Reg. Maxi. Only sixty thou on the clock, one lady owner—she was a nun—and it runs like a blooming Swiss watch. I could do you a deal if—"

Mrs. Pargeter managed to stop the flow, apologising that she really wasn't looking for a car, but needed to contact Mr. Wilson urgently. Did Mickey's Motors, by any chance, have the Hanover Square number?

He obliged and their conversation concluded amicably with assurances on his part that, if she ever needed some "really ace wheels," he had the biggest selection south of the Thames and could do her a deal that'd be grounds for having him certified.

Mrs. Pargeter rang the number he had given her and was answered by a girl with vowels of pure Waterford Crystal. "Ridleigh's. Good morning. Can I help you?"

"I'd like to speak to Mr. Wilson, please."

"One moment. I believe he may be in conference with a client who's just arrived from the Middle East. I'll see if he's free."

A tasteful burst of Vivaldi played down the line and then another voice, even more cut-glass than the first, said, "Hello. Mr. Wilson's office."

"Oh, I wondered if I could speak to him, please."

"I'm not sure that he's free. Who is it calling?"

Mrs. Pargeter recognised the formula. Mr. Wilson was sitting right next door to the secretary, but he would only be free if it was a caller he wished to speak to. An Arab prince seeking a fleet of little runabouts for his wives, perhaps . . . ?

"My name is Mrs. Pargeter."

"Mrs. Pargeter?"

"Yes. Mrs. Melita Pargeter."

There was a silence from the other end of the phone while this information was covertly relayed. Then, instantly, another extension was picked up and a voice marinated in Eton and the Guards effused, "Mrs. Pargeter!"

"Hello, Rewind."

"Oh, erm . . ." There was an elaborate cough from the other end. "I'd rather you didn't actually use that name, if you don't mind."

"Sorry, love." She could see his point. It had been a bit tactless. A man who'd earned his nickname from the skill with which he wound back milometers would hardly want it shouted around the West End office where he sold Bentleys to Bahrain.

"Don't mention it. Perfectly natural. Instinctive reaction." Rewind Wilson boomed. "Oh, it's such a pleasure to hear you, Mrs. Pargeter. You know, I keep thinking about your husband and the things we got up to."

"So do I," she admitted, indulging in a little moment of melancholy.

"He was the best. Absolutely the best. No one to touch him in the field."

"It's nice of you to say so."

"True, dear lady. Absolutely true. Wouldn't say it if it weren't. Anyway, to what do I owe the great pleasure of your call after all these years?" But before she could reply, he went on, "Your late husband, incidentally, did ask me to give you any help that you might ever require. I would have done, anyway, out of loyalty—I only mention it so's you know how much he cared for you."

That was the one thing Mrs. Pargeter had never doubted. "Thank you, Re—Mr. Wilson," she hastily corrected herself. "In fact, there was a small favour I was going to ask you."

"Anything, dear lady, anything."

"Do you still have all your contacts in the motoring world . . . I mean, even though you've gone str—um, changed your line of business?"

"I think you'll find my contacts are as good as anyone's in the trade."

"And you still have, um . . . access to the computers?"

"You name it, Mrs. Pargeter, I'll track it down."

"Well, I am actually trying to find a specific vehicle."

"This would not be for purchase, dear lady, would it?"

"No, I'm trying to trace someone. I thought finding them through their car might be a good approach. And I remembered that there was an occasion when you gave my late husband some assistance in a somewhat similar situation . . ."

"Shall we just mention the words 'Welwyn Garden City' . . . ?" asked Rewind Wilson, with a conspiratorial wink in his voice.

"Exactly."

"Right. No problem. Fill me in on all the information you have, and I give you my word that I'll track the vehicle in question down for you."

"Thank you. Well, the car's a Fiat Uno. Only a year old. And the owner's name's Cotton. Might be in the wife's name, Theresa, or the husband's, which is Rodney."

"Fine. Do you have their address?"

"The last recorded address I have for them is . . ." And she gave her own.

"Splendid. Give me a number where I can get back to you and I'll be on to it straight away."

"Thank you so much." She gave him her telephone number.

"Incidentally, Mrs. Pargeter," he asked, once again conspiratorial, "is this in connection with a 'job'?"

"I'm sorry," she replied, suddenly glacial. "I'm afraid I don't understand what you mean."

Rewind Wilson was covered with confusion. "No, I do apologise. Silly of me. Don't know what came over me. Forget I said it. Please."

She accorded him a magnanimous, "Very well."

"I'll get back to you as soon as I can, dear lady. Can't say how long it'll be, I'm afraid—depends on the circumstances—but rest assured that I will set things in motion as quickly as possible."

"Thank you."

"Well, once again may I say what a pleasure it has been to hear from you again. And . . . erm . . ." He cleared his throat awkwardly. ". . . terribly sorry about what I said just then. Didn't want to imply . . . Hope you didn't get the idea I—"

"Think nothing of it, Mr. Wilson," said Mrs. Pargeter sweetly. "And thank you so much for your help. Goodbye."

CHAPTER FOURTEEN

Through the net curtains, whose advantages she was coming to appreciate increasingly the longer she spent in Smithy's Loam, Mrs. Pargeter saw her next-door neighbour emerge from the front door of "Cromarty" with a bucket, sponge and cloths. Not content with the daily drubbing she gave to the inside of her windows, Carole Temple was now set to punish the outside.

Mrs. Pargeter decided it was time she should do a little gentle gardening. A little gentle *front* gardening.

She went to the shed at the back and selected a hoe, an edging tool, a trowel and a trug. Those ought to cover most eventualities, she thought. The trug in particular seemed to say "gardening" to her. She remembered walking with the late Mr. Pargeter through the garden of the big house in Chigwell, carrying a trugful of flowers on many a Sunday afternoon. She had loved that garden; it was always so beautifully cared for.

Not of course that she actually had to do any of the caring herself. The late Mr. Pargeter had always ensured that her gardening efforts were restricted to cutting flowers and putting them in a trug. He organised the men who were their frequent guests to do the real work. It was surprising how happy those men had always been to do a little gardening in exchange for a few days of unobserved calm in Chigwell.

Mrs. Pargeter went round the side of the house to the front garden, and when she saw Carole Temple she called out a cheery, "Good morning."

Her neighbour froze in mid-wipe, and nodded a perfunctory "Good morning" back. Then she returned determinedly to her window-cleaning, the set of her shoulders a fierce deterrent to further conversation.

But Mrs. Pargeter was not daunted by that sort of thing. After a little tentative scrabbling with her hoe in one of the front beds, she said, "Do you do your garden yourself, Carole?"

This prompted another affronted freeze, before a reply was conceded. "Yes. My husband does most of it."

"Handy things, husbands," Mrs. Pargeter commented breezily. "I miss a good few of the things my husband used to do."

The innuendo was deliberate and, Mrs. Pargeter knew, a bit childish. But Carole Temple's stuffiness had that effect on her. She was determined to get some reaction, any reaction, out of her neighbour.

But that was apparently not the way to get it. Carole continued rubbing the glass as if she hoped to come through on the other side.

"I think I might have to get a little man in to help out." Mrs. Pargeter went on and then, realising that she was keeping the innuendo going, chuckled throatily. "Oh dear, aren't I dreadful?" she said, still trying to get a rise out of Carole.

The rubbing became even more vigorous.

"Did the Cottons do this garden themselves?"

Faced with a direct question, Carole could not stay silent without overt rudeness, so she had to reply. "Yes. Well, of course, for the last few months Theresa did it all."

She couldn't have set up a better cue for Mrs. Pargeter if she had tried. "Yes. I gather Mr. Cotton hadn't been around for some time . . . ?"

"No."

Mrs. Pargeter was not going to be deterred by monosyllables. "Got a job up North, did I hear?"

"Yes."

"Where was that exactly?"

Carole looked with slight annoyance away from her cleaning, and what she saw brought an expression of shock to her face. Mrs. Pargeter had now moved forward and was actually leaning against the dividing wall between their properties, for all the world like a gossip from a northern soap opera.

"I have no idea," Carole Temple snapped, her eyes blazing the message that Mrs. Pargeter's behaviour did not conform with the usages of Smithy's Loam.

Mrs. Pargeter, fully aware of the effect she was having, gave no sign of taking the hint. Instead, she beamed cheer-

fully and asked, "And how long ago was it he got transferred?"

Again Carole could not evade the direct question.

"I suppose about six months ago. Round March, I
think."

Ah, so the lie about promotion had been around as long
as the reality of redundancy itself.

"And did you see him much after he started work up
North, Carole?"

"Hardly at all. Presumably he was busy with the new
job."

"Yes. When you say 'hardly at all,' do you mean that,
or do you mean 'not at all'?"

"What?" Carole had now given up any attempt at polishing and was looking at her interrogator with undisguised
irritation.

"I meant, Carole love,"—Mrs. Pargeter knew exactly
how much the endearment would grate—"did you see Rod
Cotton at all after he had changed jobs?"

"Well, I think so. I think he was here for a while between
the two. I don't know, quite honestly. I mean, he wasn't
around much before." She was getting flustered, and annoyed that she was getting flustered. "I'm not the sort of
person who spends all the time minding my neighbours'
business rather than my own."

Mrs. Pargeter gave a beatific smile, as if unaware of any
possibility of sarcasm in the last remark. "No, no. Neither
am I," she agreed equably.

She still showed no signs of moving away from the wall.
Carole took her frustration out on the windows, which
squeaked with protest at their chastisement.

"Must've been lonely for Theresa . . ." Mrs. Pargeter

mused. "Stuck down here, husband away all the time. I wouldn't have liked it. My husband always had to be away a certain amount . . . you know, in connection with his business . . . and I never really felt right until he came back."

This did not seem to Carole to be worthy of reaction.

"No, I didn't like it. Still, I know there are some couples it doesn't worry . . . Some seem a lot happier to be separated than to be together . . . Depends how close they are, really, I suppose . . . how things are going between them . . ."

But if Mrs. Pargeter had hoped that this fishing would elicit any comment on the state of the Cottons' marriage, she was disappointed. Carole Temple just wrung out her cloth as if she were strangling it and attacked a top corner of the window with an air of finality.

Recognising that she had pushed as far as she dared and got as much information as she was going to get that morning, Mrs. Pargeter rubbed her hands together and moved back from the wall. "Still, haven't got time to stay here chatting all day, pleasant though it is. Things to get on with. See you soon, I'm sure. 'Bye, 'bye, love."

Again the familiarity stung Carole, whose head spun round to face her neighbour. She looked upstaged and very cross. If anyone should be curtailing this unwanted conversation, it should be her and not the person who had forced it on her.

But she was too late. Mrs. Pargeter had picked up her unused garden tools and, with a little twitch of mischief at the corners of her mouth, waved serenely, before disappearing round the side of her house.

CHAPTER FIFTEEN

In spite of his new up-market address and his new up-market business, Rewind Wilson had lost none of his old efficiency in negotiating the labyrinth of crooked passages which unites the country's car dealers. He rang back the widow of his former employer the next morning at half-past eleven.

"Mrs. Pargeter, hello," the ersatz Etonian tones rumbled. "Sorry it's taken me so long to get back to you . . ."— which was simply showing off under the circumstances—". . . but I do now have the information you require."

"About the Fiat Uno?"

"That's right. Very easy to trace, as it turned out."

"Oh?"

"Yes. I thought I might have to get the road scouts out on to it, but in fact it's with a dealer."

"With a dealer?" Mrs. Pargeter echoed, slightly puzzled.

"Yes. It was sold to a fellow in Clapham. Sid Runcorn . . . never met him, but I've heard he's a bit heavily into the old F and R . . ."

For an innocent widow in her late sixties, Mrs. Pargeter had a surprisingly comprehensive knowledge of underworld slang, but on this occasion she had to admit ignorance.

Rewind Wilson supplied an immediate gloss. "F and R—Fill-in and Respray. A lot of it done on dodgy bodywork . . . never mind the rust, slap on the filler, sand it down, couple of coats of spray—fool ninety-nine per cent of the punters any day." He suddenly recollected his new status in the motor industry. "Or so I'm told."

"What, so he's done that to the Cottons' car?" asked Mrs. Pargeter, her mind racing with images of vehicles disguised to avoid detection.

"No, no, nothing like that. I only mention it because it's the only thing I know about him. No, in this case it was a straight purchase for resale."

"You mean the Cottons sold him their car?"

"That's right. He's had his engineers look it over and it's standing out on his forecourt in Clapham with a price stuck on the windscreen."

"What kind of price?"

"What do you mean?"

"Well, compared to what the Cottons sold it for . . . ?"

Rewind Wilson dropped back instinctively into a professional defensive posture. "Of course, there would be quite a mark-up . . ."

"How much?"

"About forty per cent on this one."

"Forty per cent!"

"Well, come on, the dealer's got his overheads and it's no picnic trying to offload motors at—" Again Rewind Wilson seemed to realise that his past was encroaching, and recovered himself. "Erm, yes, I believe some of the dealers down that end of the market can be a little unscrupulous in the matter of pricing."

"Yes . . ." Mrs. Pargeter thought for a moment. "Anything unusual about this sale?"

"Unusual? I believe it was all perfectly legitimate. With a car only a year old you don't usually have to do much in the way of cosmetics . . . you know, unless it's an insurance writeoff and you've got to weld the chassis and — or so I believe. I mean, so I have heard from operators in that kind of area of the market," he concluded cautiously.

"I didn't mean anything illegal. I just meant was there anything odd about it, anything that struck Mr. Runcorn as odd . . . ?"

"Ah, I'm with you. Well, there were only two things he mentioned. One, the call about the car was from way off his usual patch. I mean, that address is down near Dorking, isn't it? Sid rarely strays out of South London."

"Then why did he this time?"

"Because the car was such a bargain."

"Really?"

"Yes. That's why he could make such a healthy markup. She was asking way below the current price guide, so he didn't mind a bit of travel to pick it up."

"Mr. Runcorn picked the car up himself?"

"Yes."

"Hmm. What would it suggest to you, Re—" Mrs. Pargeter cleared her throat to cover the gaffe, "Mr. Wilson . . . you know, when someone tries to sell a car below its market value?"

"Could be various reasons. Might be just they're clueless, don't know a thing about motors . . . Or could be for a quick sale . . ."

Mrs. Pargeter preferred the second explanation. It fitted in well with the rest of her thinking about Theresa Cotton's disappearance. A quick sale of the car to a dealer from outside the area—probably randomly selected from the Yellow Pages—would raise less questions in Smithy's Loam than a local transaction. And the lowered price was probably just an incentive to make sure that Theresa's chosen dealer rose to the bait.

"Mr. Wilson, I wonder . . . could you get a little more information for me . . . ?"

"No problem at all, my dear Mrs. Pargeter."

"Are you sure I'm not keeping you from your work?"

"No, no, I've got a couple of sheikhs in the outer office, but they can wait."

"Now, I shouldn't be stopping you from—"

"Don't think about it. They're having such fun propositioning my secretaries, offering ever-increasing inducements for unlikely personal services, that they won't notice the time."

"How do the secretaries react?" asked Mrs. Pargeter, intrigued.

"Oh, they think it's enormous fun. Finishing schools may not do much in the educational line, but they at least teach them how to deal with that kind of thing."

"Ah."

"Anyway, what was the further information you required, Mrs. Pargeter?"

"It's a few fine details. I'd like to know whether Mr.

Runcorn dealt just with Mrs. Cotton or whether he dealt with the husband too. I'd like to know exactly what day and what time he collected the car. Oh, and I'd like a physical description of Mr. Runcorn."

"Very well, Mrs. Pargeter. I'll call you back as soon as possible."

If Rewind Wilson had any curiosity as to why she wanted this information, he restrained it. He had no wish to make another gaffe like the one at the end of their previous conversation.

He rang back within the half-hour.

"Yes, I have it all, Mrs. Pargeter. Sid Runcorn had no dealings with anyone other than Mrs. Cotton. She was the one who rang him and offered the car for sale. She fixed the time for him to come and collect it, and she it was who let him in when he arrived."

"When was this?"

"Last Monday. Week ago yesterday."

As she had thought. "And what time did he arrive?"

"About seven in the evening. He'd gone down by train, you see, because he was going to be driving the Fiat back."

This again supported her conjectures. So did the physical description of Sid Runcorn. He was of medium height, with a beard that he never trimmed, and his customary working clothes were a grubby navy-blue overall and a woolly hat. In other words, he was Theresa Cotton's second bearded visitor on her last day in Smithy's Loam.

"How long did he stay at the house?"

"Not long. He looked at the car in the garage, took it round the block for a test-drive, then handed over the money, and went off. He was very chuffed. Beautiful little motor, he said. Low mileage, really been looked after."

"And what, did he give Mrs. Cotton a cheque?"

"No, no, cash. All Sid Runcorn's deals are cash," was the firm reply.

"How much was the price?"

Rewind Wilson told her. Though apparently little for a car of the age and condition of the Cottons' Fiat, it was still a lot for the average housewife to have loose in cash about her house.

"And, Mr. Wilson, when Mr. Runcorn left, he didn't take Mrs. Cotton with him, did he?"

"What?" This time he could not keep the curiosity out of his voice. "No, of course not. Why should he do that?"

"Oh, no reason. No, don't worry about it. Look, Re—" Oh dear, doing it again. ". . . Mr. Wilson, thank you enormously for all your help."

"Think absolutely nothing of it, dear lady. It's a mere drop in the ocean, compared to all your late husband did for me. You know, if I hadn't been working with him, I'd never have been able to afford to set myself up in my current line."

"Oh, well, I'm so glad. Always liked to help others, Mr. Pargeter did."

"Yes, he was a real Robin Hood."

"Except that Robin Hood was a thief." Mrs. Pargeter reproved him mischievously.

Rewind Wilson was once again swamped in embarrassment. "I'm so sorry. In no way did I wish to imply that your late—"

Mrs. Pargeter cut through all this. "Don't you worry. I was only joking. Listen, thanks a million. I'll get out of your hair now, and let you get on with the sheikhs."

"They'll be no problem."

"Do they haggle about the price?" she asked, curious.

"Good heavens, no. With them and Rollers, it's not a question of price, it's a question of how many. Oh no, they're prepared to pay for what they want."

Mrs. Pargeter giggled. "Does that go for your secretaries' services, too?"

"It certainly does. Girl on Reception went out to dinner with one of our Middle Eastern clients last week . . ."

"Oh?"

"Came in this morning driving a brand-new Porsche."

"Really?"

"Mind you, she reckoned she earned every last hub-cap. Still, we don't need to go into the details of that, do we?"

"No. No, I suppose we don't," Mrs. Pargeter agreed, rather wistfully.

She now had three new pieces of information.

First, the appearance of Theresa Cotton's second bearded visitor was explained.

Second, on her last evening in "Acapulco," Theresa Cotton had a great deal of cash with her.

And, third, she didn't leave her house at the time Fiona Burchfield-Brown had assumed she had left.

In fact, no one had seen Theresa Cotton leave her house at all.

CHAPTER SIXTEEN

Mrs. Pargeter decided she would have a little walk before lunch. She always tried to have at least one walk a day; she knew how important it was for people to keep mobile as they got older. And exercise, she hoped, might slow down her not-unattractive tendency towards plumpness.

Also, she found walking very conducive to constructive thought.

She determined that, rather than taking the customary route from her front door, she would explore round the back of the house. There was a high gate in the neat fencing at the end of her garden, and she had not yet had time to discover what lay beyond it. She did not entertain romantic notions of finding a secret garden like that in her favourite childhood book, but she still felt a little buzz of excitement at the thought of the unknown.

As she walked down the path, she noticed how ragged the back garden had grown even in the brief period of her residence. All gardens look ragged in late autumn, but somehow the other householders of Smithy's Loam had disciplined nature firmly to conform to their high standards.

Mrs. Pargeter decided she must organise the services of a gardener. Not, she proudly asserted to herself, because she gave a damn about what her neighbours thought; simply because she liked living in pleasant surroundings.

For a moment she wondered whether she might be able to contact some of the men who proved so green-fingered during their enforced seclusion at the big house in Chigwell, but she quickly concluded that it might be a little difficult to arrange. No, better to apply for help locally. And asking advice on where to find a good gardener could be a useful excuse for paying a call on other Smithy's Loam residents when the need arose.

The gate had metal bolts at top and bottom, but these were not locked. It opened easily, and Mrs. Pargeter found herself on a tarmacked path which ran along the line of fencing at the back of the houses. Across the path was a thin band of woodland, some fifty metres wide, beyond which, through the stripped trees of autumn, she could see the undulations of a golf course. This access to open space for the walking of dogs—or even for the playing of golf—was another of the features of which the original Smithy's Loam brochure had made much.

The strip of woodland was frequented by rabbits, squirrels and the occasional flasher, but Mrs. Pargeter's sensibilities were not challenged that morning. (In fact, if they had been, she would have coped better than many women of her age. On one occasion a few years previously, when walking along the dunes at Littlehampton West Beach, she had been confronted by a twenty-year-old man determined to show her his all. Without breaking her stride, Mrs. Pargeter had stared at what was on offer, sniffed, said, "I've seen better," and continued her walk.)

The path curved round the back gardens of all the houses in Smithy's Loam. Each neat fence had its own neat gate, though on the tops of some, barbed wire or metal spikes had been affixed to deter intruders.

At the apex of the close the woodland gave way to a long wall, topped with broken glass. As Mrs. Pargeter walked along the narrow passage between the high fencing and this wall, she conjectured what might lie behind it. However, she was not kept in ignorance for long, because the path opened out into what proved to be the service road behind the Shopping Parade, and she could see at the entrance to the walled enclosure a sign identifying it as a local dairy depot.

She continued her circuit, passing along the end of the Parade, past the threatened coffee shop, turning left on to the main road and then into Smithy's Loam and back home.

The excursion had taken her less than five minutes. Not long enough, really, to count as a constitutional. Certainly not long enough to have any counteractive effect on her potential weight problem.

But quite long enough to stimulate some very useful thoughts.

The back access to the path meant that one could leave "Acapulco" without being seen from the other houses in Smithy's Loam. And the fact that the bolts on the gate had not been closed from the inside suggested that someone might quite recently have departed by that route.

But the path offered opportunities for arrivals as well as departures. Though, from what she had seen of them, it seemed unlikely that they ever would, the residents of Smithy's Loam could pay each other clandestine visits that way.

And, of course, it need not just be other residents who took advantage of this means of access.

More than ever, Mrs. Pargeter felt the urgency to make contact with either Theresa or Rod Cotton.

The police, of course, have departments specialising in the location of Missing Persons, but one of the enduring legacies of her life with the late Mr. Pargeter was a marked reluctance to contact the police when any possible alternative presented itself. They were, Mrs. Pargeter thought in her altruistic way, very busy people and, if one could avoid adding to their work-load, one was behaving in a properly public-spirited way.

The late Mr. Pargeter's address book, however, did offer an alternative means of setting a search in motion, and it was that number that his widow punched up as soon as she returned after her brief constitutional.

"Hello. Mason De Vere Detective Agency."

"What!"

The voice, female, righteously Welsh, repeated, "*I said* this is the Mason De Vere Detective Agency."

"Oh. Could I speak to Mr. Mason, please?"

"Can I say who wants him?"

"Well, you see, my husband—"

"Oh, I see, it's matrimonial." The Welsh voice picked up speed as it spoke. "Don't you worry, here at the agency we're very good at those cases. You just tell us what he looks like and we'll find out what he's been up to. We'll catch the grubby bastard with his trousers down, you can rest assured of that."

"No, I'm sorry, I'm talking about my *late* husband."

"Don't talk to me about 'late.' I know all about that, too. Oh yes, always coming in when the supper's burnt to a frazzle, with some excuse about 'something having come up at the office'—and we all know what it was that came up, don't we? You don't have to tell me about that."

"But I—"

"And you know exactly where they've been, don't you? Oh, they no longer have lipstick on their collars or come in smelling of perfume, do they? Too subtle for that, I *don't* think. No, now it's coming in smelling of deodorant and aftershave . . . I mean, I ask you—who puts on deodorant and aftershave just when they're leaving the office? Unless they've got something to hide, eh? And then there's always the bunch of flowers, isn't there? Showing just how guilty the bastards are. Imagining the little wife's so bloody stupid they fob her off with a bunch of flowers. Huh."

The righteous Welsh voice paused to breathe, and Mrs. Pargeter took the opportunity to stem this anti-masculine tirade. "No, I'm sorry, you've got it wrong. I'm talking about my *late* husband. My *dead* husband."

"Oh. You actually killed the bastard, did you?" asked the Welsh voice with a note of admiration.

"No. My name is Mrs. Pargeter. Mr. Mason used to work with my husband. And I would be most grateful if you could put me through to Mr. Mason."

"Oh." The monosyllable sounded disappointed that there was no husband-murder to prompt the call. "Very well."

The line went silent while the identity of his caller was conveyed to Mr. Mason, and then a deep, mournful voice took over the phone. "Mrs. Pargeter, what an enormous pleasure."

Someone who had never heard the voice before might have suspected irony, so at odds with the contents of the speech was its lugubrious delivery. But Mrs. Pargeter knew the voice's owner and his funereal manner from way back.

"Truffler, lovely to hear you, too."

"Hmm. It's really wonderful to be called 'Truffler' again. Makes me feel quite young." This was delivered in the tones of a man who had just had his appeal against the death sentence rejected.

"But what's with all this 'Detective Agency'? Have you gone legit?"

"Yes," Truffler Mason admitted apologetically. "Really, after Mr. Pargeter was out of the business, it all got a bit predictable. And I thought, goodness, I've got all these qualifications—why don't I turn them to good account? Anyway, the whole emphasis of the old business has changed. Used to be plenty of work looking for missing people. Now most of the big boys just want help in making people go missing. Never my style, that."

"No."

"Nor Mr. Pargeter's."

"No."

"Anyway, I find it's all working out rather well," said Truffler Mason, sounding as if he'd just heard of the death of all his family in a motorway pile-up.

"And who's De Vere?"

"De Vere?"

"In the agency's name?"

"Oh, that De Vere. There isn't one."

"Then why use the name?"

"First few weeks I started, it was just the 'Mason Agency,' but I kept getting calls from people reckoning I had the ear of some Grandmaster or something and could get them into a Lodge or wore an apron or had a funny handshake . . . I don't know. So I thought it'd be simpler if I just changed the name. And De Vere added a bit of class. It's raised the class of the clients no end."

"Oh. Good."

"Anyway, what can I do for you, Mrs. Pargeter? Anything you ask shall be done. You know, without Mr. Pargeter's training, I couldn't have begun to think of setting up on my own."

"No. Well, actually, Truffler, it is Missing Persons work."

"Good. I enjoy that," he commented in the voice of a man three minutes fifty-nine seconds into the four-minute warning.

"There are two people I need to track down. Husband and wife."

She gave him the sketchy details she knew of Rod and Theresa Cotton's lives. He asked a few unlikely supplementary questions and then said he would do his best. He was far too professional to ask the reason why she wanted the couple traced.

"Leave it with me, Mrs. Pargeter. I'll get back to you as soon as I've got a whisper."

"Thanks, Truffler. I knew I could rely on you."

"Any time. Anything. Oh, and . . ." His voice grew even deeper, conspiratorially gloomy. "I hope you didn't have any trouble with the girl on the switchboard," he murmured.

"Well, um . . . no. She was . . . maybe a bit strange."

"Mm. You got to make allowances, though. She is just coming to the end of a particularly sticky divorce."

"Oh, really?" said Mrs. Pargeter. "I'd never have guessed."

CHAPTER SEVENTEEN

The same efficient American voice answered the telephone. "Church of Utter Simplicity."

"Oh, hello. I wonder if you could help me . . . ?" Mrs. Pargeter was playing for time; she had not yet worked out what was going to be her best approach.

"Yes. And what sort of help was it that you required?"

"Well, I suppose . . . spiritual help."

The woman on the switchboard was unfazed by this request. No doubt, Mrs. Pargeter assumed, places with names like the Church of Utter Simplicity were used to dealing with telephonic enquiries on spiritual matters. "I'll put you through to Brother Michael," the American voice said. This was, in a way, what Mrs. Pargeter had wanted to happen, but now it was happening, it caused her some anxiety. She had already had two telephone conversations with Brother Michael. If he recognised her voice, his suspicions might be aroused.

On the other hand, she had not mentioned her name on either occasion. She decided to identify herself immediately and hope that, out of context, he would not make the association.

"Good afternoon, my name is Mrs. Pargeter," she announced boldly, as soon as the fruity voice had answered.

"Well, Mrs. Pargeter, and what can I do for you?"

"It's difficult . . ." she began, still shaping her plan of campaign.

"The Church," he pronounced pontifically, "is here to be an ever-present help in time of trouble." Whether he was referring to the Church of Utter Simplicity or to some larger concept of the Christian Church was not clear, but Mrs. Pargeter rather suspected it was the former.

"Yes. The fact is . . ." She edged forward cautiously, remembering the tone of Theresa Cotton's unposted letter. ". . . that in recent years I have become increasingly dissatisfied with the kind of materialism I see all around me."

"Our Lord," Brother Michael intoned, "came into the world, like us, with nothing. And when we leave the world, we will leave it with nothing. Does it not therefore seem irrelevant to set store by the riches of this world?"

"Well, yes, that's exactly what I've been thinking," Mrs. Pargeter lied. The late Mr. Pargeter, she knew, would forgive her in the circumstances, although what she said went very strongly against one of the basic tenets of his life. He could never have been described as a greedy man, but he had always had—and encouraged in his wife—a proper sense of the value of material things.

"And I don't know . . ." she went on with increasing confidence. Now she had a line to follow, the words came with no problem. "The more things one accumulates, the more unimportant they all seem. And the more complicated everything gets."

"Indeed," Brother Michael asserted eagerly, pouncing on the cue. "And the more one feels in need of a more simple life."

"Exactly."

"This is a conclusion I myself and certain like-minded brethren reached some twenty years ago. And it was from that that the Church of Utter Simplicity was born."

"Yes. I really would like to know more about your Church."

"You are welcome to any information you may require. If, that is to say," he admonished, "you ask in a spirit of genuine enquiry after Eternal Truth."

Mrs. Pargeter crossed her fingers. "Oh yes, of course I do."

"Am I to understand that you are considering the possibility of joining our church?"

"Well, I had thought of it. I mean, I'd certainly like to know more about the set-up. There isn't an age limit on entry, is there?" she added anxiously. "I'm not exactly in the first flush of youth."

"There are no restrictions on entry to the Church of Utter Simplicity," Brother Michael boomed. "The only qualification is a heart empty of acquisitiveness and a mind ready to devote itself to the contemplation of the Almighty Simplicity of God."

"Yes. Yes, well, I think I could probably manage that," Mrs. Pargeter lied again.

"I must ask," Brother Michael pressed on, "just a few details about yourself. You know, it would be time-wasting to arrange an interview if there were some obvious reason why we would not suit."

What a strange way of putting it, Mrs. Pargeter thought. In her own mind, she had already reached the conclusion that what wouldn't make someone "suit" was a completely empty bank balance. She had a feeling that the Church of Utter Simplicity, though emphasising that people could *take* nothing with them, would not welcome aspirant members who *brought* nothing with them. But perhaps she was being overcynical.

"First," Brother Michael continued, "what is your marital status?"

"I am widowed," she replied in appropriately subdued tones.

He produced an uninterested reflex condolence. "So your problem is not a husband who keeps lavishing worldly goods upon you?"

"Oh no. Mind you, he did in the past. He was very lavish, the late Mr. Pargeter. But now, I'm afraid, I have to do most of the lavishing on myself."

"You are at least fortunate—even though in the unhappy state of widowhood—that you do not have to worry too much about money."

"Oh, goodness, no. That's not a problem." She stopped herself, and continued soberly. "Well, yes, it is a problem—that is what makes me so materialistic, which is the cause of my spiritual problems. But the lack of money is not a problem in the conventional sense."

"No, no," said Brother Michael judiciously. And then he went straight on to arrange an interview for the next morning. The "just a few details about yourself" seemed to have become less important once the health of her bank balance had been established.

Or, again, Mrs. Pargeter asked herself, was she letting her natural scepticism get the better of her?

CHAPTER EIGHTEEN

~~~~~~

Dunstridge Manor had presumably in its time been the home of the Lord of the Manor of Dunstridge, but now it looked like a private school. So many such buildings became private schools when the depredations of death duties ousted family owners that the architectural style now says "private school" rather than "manor house" to the casual onlooker.

And at Dunstridge Manor this impression was reinforced by a scattering of low, apparently prefabricated buildings around the central Tudor pile. (It is a rule, quickly observed by prospective parents doing the rounds, that in all English private schools the majority of classrooms shall be in prefabricated buildings. A secondary rule supports the thesis that, the higher the fees are, the tattier these prefabricated buildings shall be.)

The Manor House, or "private school," was in good repair, and so were the low prefabricated buildings, offering the hope to an inspecting parent that the fees might be quite reasonable. But such an inspection was not the purpose of Mrs. Pargeter's mission. Once she was out of her hired limousine, she merely noted the condition of the buildings, observed evidence of well-organised agricultural activity in the surrounding area, and tugged at the long wrought-iron bell-pull beside the studded oak door.

After a pause, the door was opened by a tallish man of indeterminate age, who wore a cassock of some rough dark blue material. He had black-framed glasses and a straggling beard. His hair had that unrubbed-tobacco texture of hair that could do with a wash.

He identified himself as "Brother Brian," and led the way across the stone-flagged hall towards a pointed doorway. As she followed, Mrs. Pargeter received the distinct impression that it wasn't only his hair that needed washing. The fumes of ancient sweat assailed her nostrils.

This Mrs. Pargeter did not like. She was aware that Man created the deodorant, but she liked to feel that the act had been performed under God's direction. She did not subscribe to any fundamentalist view that, if God hadn't intended people to smell, then He wouldn't have given them sweaty armpits. If that was one of the beliefs of the Church whose premises she had just entered, then she thought it was taking Simplicity too far.

The hall they crossed could have been magnificent, but wasn't. It needed thick rugs on the flagstones, heavy brocade curtains at the windows, ancestral portraits on the wall, maybe the odd stag's head, stuffed pike or spray of halberds. Instead, no doubt in accordance with the precepts of Simplicity, there were thin cotton check curtains, chipboard notice-boards, metal filing cabinets and rows of the sort of coat-hooks found in municipal swimming baths.

But it was all clean and tidy. When they entered, two girls in their twenties, sleeves of their navy blue cassocks rolled up, were polishing the magnificent oak banisters of the staircase. They showed no interest in the new arrival. Neither looked up. The face of the one Mrs. Pargeter could see was blank. Not blank in rapt contemplation of the Almighty Simplicity, but blank as if devoid of thought.

Through the doorway, Mrs. Pargeter and her rancid usher found themselves in an office. Here, too, all was neat, but, again, no concession had been made to the beauty of the room. Its stately lines were broken by more metal cabinets, and its finely panelled walls obscured by more notice-boards, as well as some rather unattractively printed texts. These were of the not-quite-biblical variety popular in the late sixties and early seventies. They even included, Mrs. Pargeter noted with distaste, *Desiderata*.

The office equipment was all very up-to-date, though its anonymous beige plastic casings provided another jarring contrast to the ancient elegance of the room. Behind the word processor keyboard and adjacent to the modern switchboard sat a woman with faded blonde hair and rimless glasses which accentuated the paleness of her eyes. Her perfunctory "Good morning. Mrs. Pargeter, is it?" identified her as the American voice which took spiritual enquiries so much in its stride.

"Brother Michael is busy on the telephone at the moment. Would you like to sit down, please, until he's free."

Though phrased as a question, the sentence had no interrogative quality; it was an order.

The chair on which Mrs. Pargeter sat was again unnecessarily functional. A tubular steel office chair. Like
everything else she had seen in the building, it aggressively denounced the temptations of materialism. Too
much so. Mrs. Pargeter knew, from her own experience,
that, for less money, the Manor House could have been
furnished with more congenial second-hand stuff. But
then the intrusion of a little taste wouldn't have given
off the same "Look at us—aren't we being unmateri-
alistic?" message.

As soon as she was seated, Brother Brian, without saying
anything, turned on his heel and padded off across the hall.
As he did so, Mrs. Pargeter noticed that the bottoms of
grubby jeans and stained trainers showed beneath the hem
of his cassock. They seemed of a piece with the rest of his
image.

Though he had gone, Brother Brian seemed, vindic-
tively, to have left his smell behind him. Mrs. Pargeter
wrinkled her nose in distaste.

The bloodless American woman opposite tapped at her
keyboard, uninterested in the visitor. Through a window
two navy-cassocked figures could be seen listlessly splitting
logs with axes. From somewhere in the recesses of the house
a recorder or tin whistle was playing *Morning Has Broken*
without expression.

Something on the desk buzzed. Without looking away
from her screen, the American woman said, "He's ready
for you now," and waved Mrs. Pargeter across the room.

The door, like others in the house, was oak with a
pointed top, but its surface was insensitively spoiled by a
taped-on notice, on which felt-penned letters read:

BROTHER MICHAEL
Spiritual enquiries
between 2:00 and 4:00 p.m. only.

Mrs. Pargeter supposed she was privileged, as an outsider, to be making her enquiry in the morning. If—and heaven forbid—she ever joined the Church of Utter Simplicity, then she would have to restrict her spiritual anxieties to two hours in the afternoon like everyone else.

She knocked, heard the fruity voice bellow "Come!" and walked in.

CHAPTER NINETEEN

Mrs. Pargeter had dressed carefully for the encounter. She wore a silk dress of a rather vibrant purple, which emphasised the voluptuousness of her figure. Over her shoulders was slung one of her better minks, and she wore the diamond-and-garnet necklace, bracelet and earring set which the late Mr. Pargeter had given her as a reward for her patience during a long absence when his work had taken him to Monte Carlo. She knew that the ensemble was over-the-top everyday wear for anyone other than a very successful romantic novelist, but it had been chosen quite deliberately, as had her arrival by limousine, to see whether it would have any effect.

She was instantly rewarded. As he rose to greet her,

Brother Michael's eyes moved straight to the necklace, then took in the bracelet and the rest of the ensemble.

"Sit you down," he said in the same charmless, hectoring manner he had used on the phone.

He wore the uniform navy blue cassock, and there was about him an overpowering masculinity. Not the masculinity that stirs sexual attraction, but the masculinity which manifests itself in large features, huge splayed hands, bushy eyebrows and thick hair in nostrils and ears. He was about sixty, a little portly and balding. The hair that remained on his head was still black, though the odd hairs missed by careless shaving were white.

(How was it, Mrs. Pargeter often wondered, that some men could manage always to miss the same bit when shaving? She could understand doing it once, even doing it a couple of days in a row, but the little tufts of quite long hairs which she often saw on otherwise smooth chins suggested a carefully planned campaign of avoidance. Most bizarre. Still, she concluded philosophically, it was probably one of those questions to which women were destined never to find the answer.)

He waited till she was seated before sitting down himself, but this seemed merely an act of conformity, not of genuine chivalry. He clasped his hands together on his desk and looked at her with the indulgence of a doctor treating a patient for recurrent hypochondria.

"Now, Mrs. Pargeter, you said on the phone that you found yourself obsessed with material things . . ."

"Yes." She launched into fabrication. "I suppose the problem is one of values, really. You know, not values in the sense of what people pay for things, or what things are worth . . . not *The Price Is Right* sort of values . . . but what things are *really* worth. Or if anything's really worth anything, come to that."

Brother Michael gave a smile of predatory sympathy. "I understand. Those who live solely by the values of this world all eventually find them to be inadequate. What is the value of money in the face of the ultimate reality, which is death? Oh, a rich man may pay for medical care that can extend his life long beyond that of a poor man, but no man yet has been rich enough to postpone death for ever."

"No. I know that. And I suppose, as my own death gets nearer . . ."

Brother Michael did not offer the token contesting of this statement which most people would have provided.

". . . as my own death gets nearer, I think more about that kind of thing. You know, where are my real values . . . ? What is life really about . . . ?"

"And why are you here . . . ?" Brother Michael supplied.

Mrs. Pargeter thought it would be just as well if she didn't give a truthful answer to that one. "Exactly. And sometimes, you know, I wish I could just shed all the trappings of wealth and concentrate on things that really matter."

Brother Michael made an awkwardly expansive gesture. "That is what we are here for. The Church of Utter Simplicity was formed for those who feel the needs you describe."

"Yes, how was the Church actually formed?" asked Mrs. Pargeter, thus condemning herself to a full twenty minutes of the history of the movement.

It had been, as she had suspected, founded in the Sixties,

and in Brother Michael's exposition, along with the biblical overtones, were references to "doing one's own thing with God," "letting God into one's own space" and "joining hands in the peace and love of God."

It was another example of how the carefree non-materialism of the Sixties has been channelled into the hard-nosed businesses of the Eighties. The unfettered world of rock music developed, through price-cutting record outlets, into a multimillion-pound leisure industry. The woolly principles of the ecology movement were groomed into companies making "natural" cosmetic products. And the Church of Utter Simplicity channelled the drifting spirit of Woodstock into the discipline of organised religion.

All these organisations were doing the same thing, playing on the guilt of those people who had grown up through the values of the Sixties and now felt embarrassed by their middle-class materialism. And all of them demonstrated the eternal history of business—that the urge to make money is a permanent force, which will adapt itself to whatever happens to be current at any given moment.

When Brother Michael reached the end of—or at least a paragraph-break in—his peroration, Mrs. Pargeter asked innocently, "And how is it all funded?"

He was not embarrassed by the question. Clearly it was one he had been faced with and dealt with on numerous occasions. However, the vehemence with which he answered suggested that he might be anticipating disagreement.

"Well, of course, we do sell some produce from the estate, but the majority of our income comes from voluntary contributions."

"Oh? And how are those voluntary contributions made?"

"Novices who join the Church make over much of their wealth to us."

He responded immediately to her raised eyebrow. This, too, was an objection he had encountered before. "When I say 'make over to us,' of course I do not mean that it's made over to any individual. The money goes into the charitable trust set up to run the Church."

"Oh, I see."

"It would hardly be appropriate," he joked heavily, "for the novices to give up all their worldly goods simply so that the leaders of the Church could live the life of Reilly."

"No. No, it wouldn't." Mrs. Pargeter paused. She wondered whether it was the moment to change tack. After all, the last thing she wanted was to become a novice of the Church of Utter Simplicity. She was only there in an investigative capacity. "As it happens," she continued casually, "I heard about the Church through a friend."

"Oh?" The priest—or whatever he called himself . . . probably just "Brother," Mrs. Pargeter reflected—was instantly alert, anticipating trouble.

"Yes, a friend called Theresa Cotton."

At the name the black eyebrows drew together into one bristling line, like a particularly noxious caterpillar.

Mrs. Pargeter wondered for a moment whether she had overstepped the mark, but it soon became clear that Brother Michael's anger was directed not at her but at her supposed friend.

"Theresa Cotton is not, I am afraid, a name that is heard with great enthusiasm within these walls. She misled us into believing that she would be joining us as a novice."

"Sister Camilla."

"That is correct. She was—" The eyebrows grew even

bushier as a new thought struck him. "Was it you? Were you the one who rang up asking for her?"

No point in denial. "Yes, it was me."

But this did not divert his anger from Theresa either. "She left us in the lurch. We had made plans for her joining the Church. We had set up her Becoming Ceremony . . ."

"Yes, she mentioned that. I didn't quite understand what she meant."

"Before you can be a part of the Church," he explained with limited patience, "you have to *become* a member of the Church."

"And once you are a member of the Church, what do you do then?"

"I'm sorry?"

"Well, having *become*, what do you do after that? Do you just *be*?"

"Yes. From then on you *are*."

"Oh." Mrs. Pargeter nodded wisely, as if that explained everything. "Erm, one thing that did interest me," she continued, "was something Theresa said about how one prepared oneself for entry to the Church."

"Yes?" The question was guarded. He became very self-protective each time Theresa Cotton's name was mentioned.

"She said something about having to clear one's mind of resentments and grudges . . ."

"That is certainly what we recommend. It is ideal that one should come to one's Becoming Ceremony with a mind receptive to God, a mind uncluttered by worldly thoughts and aggravations."

"Yes, of course. And what," she asked cautiously, "would be the best way of getting oneself into that state of mind?"

"We always recommend direct confrontation."

"With whom? I mean who do you confront?"

"Anyone towards whom you feel guilt or resentment."

"Oh, I see. You sort of talk to them and get it off your chest . . ."

"That is correct. Since you are leaving that part of the world behind, it is important to clear any bad feeling that there may be between you and any of your fellow creatures."

"Oh, yes, right. I'm all in favour of that. And when would you recommend doing this . . . you know, the clearing the air business . . . ?"

"It is best that it should be done as near to the time of joining the Church as possible. Otherwise old wounds could be reopened and the resentments could grow rather than diminish."

"Yes, yes, I suppose they could," Mrs. Pargeter agreed thoughtfully.

What Brother Michael had said confirmed the information in Theresa Cotton's letter. Immediately before her disappearance she had engineered a series of "confrontations" with people against whom she harboured resentments.

Or who harboured resentments against her, perhaps . . . ?

Mrs. Pargeter suddenly recalled Fiona Burchfield-Brown saying that Theresa had come to see her at about six o'clock on the Monday evening before she vanished. How many other people in Smithy's Loam had received similar visits? And what had been the subjects of the conversations during those visits?

Mrs. Pargeter would make it her business to get answers to those questions.

It was clear that Brother Michael himself had not been

thoroughly successful in ridding his own mind of resentments and grudges. "I'm afraid your friend Theresa Cotton," he snapped suddenly, "let us down pretty badly. Particularly financially. There was some maintenance work on the roof here which we've recently had started on the promise of certain moneys from her."

"I'm so sorry. Well, I wouldn't like to think that my being a friend of hers might inhibit my chances of—"

"My dear Mrs. Pargeter, of course not." Brother Michael was suddenly as near as he ever got to charm. The effect of the limousine and the jewellery had not diminished. "No, no. We would be delighted if you wish to consider giving up your life for God."

"Yes." And not just my life, thought Mrs. Pargeter—that'd be the smallest part of it. "Well, look, obviously I'll want to think about all this . . ."

"Naturally. Would you like me to show you round the premises, give you an idea of the sort of works we do here?"

Why was it people of that sort always talked about "works" rather than "work," she reflected, before replying, "That's very kind, but I really must say no. Keep that pleasure for another visit. You've already given me so much food for thought this morning."

"Good. I am glad to hear it. And may I express the hope that God will make your thoughts grow and come nearer to His Almighty Simplicity."

Mrs. Pargeter was not quite sure of the proper response to a remark like that. She made do with, "Oh, thank you."

"Let me give you some literature about our beliefs and the works that we do here." He thrust a couple of colour-printed booklets into her hands. On the front of each were the words "Church of Utter Simplicity" and a logo which featured a cross, a fish, a tree and a couple of rabbits.

Then Brother Michael led her to the door and opened it. "God bless you," he said, as if he were the only person on earth with franchising rights in divine benison. "You will be in my prayers."

Yuk, thought Mrs. Pargeter. Being in Brother Michael's prayers was the last place on earth she wanted to be.

In fact, she decided firmly, she didn't want to have anything to do with the Church of Utter Simplicity ever again. She had never encountered a supposedly spiritual institution that she found so supremely dispiriting.

In the back of the limousine, as it returned her to Smithy's Loam, Mrs. Pargeter thought about the visit. The Church of Utter Simplicity was a deeply unappealing place, peopled by deeply unappealing people, but she did not think anyone there could have had anything to do with the disappearance of Theresa Cotton.

No, they wanted her money too much. Clearly the non-arrival of Theresa's promised contribution had put them into some difficulties.

Mrs. Pargeter glanced idly at the booklets she had been given. The activities of the members of the Church of Utter Simplicity looked as drab and charmless as she had expected. It seemed inconceivable that anyone could go voluntarily into that kind of tedium.

She wondered for a moment whether the whole set-up was crooked, but decided not. There was certainly a lot of hypocrisy there, and plenty of ironic counterpoint to be seen between unworldly ideals and money-grabbing practice. But she didn't think it was actually criminal—and, thanks to the life she had led with the late Mr. Pargeter, she did have a finely attuned nose for criminality in any form.

In the open booklet on her lap she saw a picture of Brother Brian leading a prayer-meeting of colourless men and women in blue cassocks, all linking hands round a large tree.

Ugh! Apart from the nauseous idea of such a get-together, Brother Brian's smell seemed suddenly still to be with her, as if it clung to her mink. She took out a little perfume spray and filled the back of the car with *Obsession*.

Then she looked again at the photograph. Tall, scruffy, bearded. Could Brother Brian have been Theresa Cotton's first bearded visitor on the afternoon of her disappearance?

It was certainly worth investigating.

CHAPTER TWENTY

Mrs. Pargeter was glad of her mink when the limousine dropped her back at Smithy's Loam. Winter had decided to make an entrance and the cold stung her cheeks as she walked to her front door. The disquiet that had been building inside her for some days was now hardening into a more positive anxiety. Soon she would have to take action.

Of course, she had taken some action already. Truffler Mason had been set in motion, and would be painstakingly working through his system trying to trace Rod and Theresa Cotton.

One of them, Mrs. Pargeter reckoned, he was in with a good chance of finding.

Making contact with the other, though, she was beginning to fear might be more difficult.

She shuddered, then pulled herself together and made a phone call to Bedford.

The second cars of Smithy's Loam were fairly reliable indicators of the presence or absence of their owners. If the second car was in the drive, the relevant wife was usually in. Though occasional forays on foot were made to the Shopping Parade or for walks on the golf course, most expeditions from the close were motorised.

The Range Rover was parked outside "High Bushes," so Mrs. Pargeter felt safe in assuming that Fiona Burchfield-Brown was in. Once again she felt a surge of irritation at the sight of the car. It was so typical of everything she had heard about Alexander Burchfield-Brown. He'd have to have a Range Rover round here, she thought, need the four-wheel drive to negotiate the notorious slopes of Sainsbury's car park.

Still, it wasn't the moment for spleen. It was time to check whether Theresa Cotton's first bearded visitor had indeed been Brother Brian.

Mrs. Pargeter put her mink coat back on and picked up the booklets she had been given at the Church of Utter Simplicity.

Fiona Burchfield-Brown ushered her willingly enough into her kitchen. The chaos was not quite so great as it had been before the dinner party, but there was still a sense of a losing battle against the encroachments of mess. The Labrador was still spread over more than its fair share of the floor. Newspaper was scattered over the table, and silver plates and cutlery lay about, in various stages of being cleaned.

"Alexander's family silver," Fiona indicated helplessly. "Coffee?"

Mrs. Pargeter accepted the offer, sat down comfortably at the table and produced the pretext for her visit. Had Fiona got the name of a good gardener locally? She had known the excuse would come in useful some time.

Fiona couldn't be very helpful. They did most of their gardening themselves. Alexander insisted. He said it was different if you had a proper estate; then of course you had staff. Otherwise he thought paying for a gardener was a ridiculous extravagance when Fiona was at home most of the time and could easily do the routine stuff. He mowed the lawns and did any digging that was required at the weekends.

"Oh?" said Mrs. Pargeter ingenuously. "I'd really put you down as 'gardener' people. You know, I'd have thought people who have Jacuzzis put in would be just the sort to . . ."

"Oh, yes, absolutely." Fiona smiled weakly. "I'm not sure that we *are* Jacuzzi people, actually. Do you know, those wretched little men who're supposed to be putting the thing in *still* haven't turned up. Alexander's furious. He says I'm to ring them every morning and bawl them out. Then, if they haven't arrived by the end of the week, I'm to cancel the order."

Typical man, Mrs. Pargeter reflected, running off to the safety of his office and the protection of his secretary, and leaving his wife to make all the nasty phone calls. At least she had been more fortunate. The late Mr. Pargeter had ensured that the course of her life had never been sullied by unpleasantness; he had taken care of all that kind of thing himself.

Yes, the more she heard about Alexander Burchfield-Brown, the less she liked him. Clearly, there was plenty of money around, but he seemed very disinclined to spend any of it on help for his wife around the house, preferring, it seemed, to leave all the chores to her incompetence.

"So, with regard to gardeners," Fiona went on apologetically, "I'm afraid I can't be much help. You could have a look in the newsagent's window down on the Parade. They have cards in there for that kind of thing."

"Oh, thank you very much, Fiona. That's a really good idea."

There was a slight lull in the conversation. Mrs. Pargeter knew the moment had come to turn to the real purpose of her visit.

"Fiona, you know I was asking you the other day about when Theresa left Smithy's Loam . . ."

"Mmm?" Fiona was absorbed in trying to get the polish out of the indentations of engraving on a silver plate.

"And you know you said that two bearded men came to visit her that day . . ."

"Uhuh."

Time for a little lie. "Well, would you believe, I've had another call from that man who was asking about exactly when Theresa left."

"Oh really? Goodness, he sounds a bit of a nosy parker, doesn't he?"

"Yes, almost like a jealous husband . . ." No harm in trawling for a little more information while she had the chance.

Fiona laughed. "Oh, I hardly think that would be appropriate with the Cottons. Not that way round, anyway."

Mrs. Pargeter was straight on to it. "What do you mean?"

Fiona Burchfield-Brown quickly covered over the lapse.

117

"Nothing, nothing. So what did this chap want to know?" she asked, adroitly redirecting the conversation.

"He was asking about these two men who visited Theresa that day. Now that really *does* sound like a jealous husband, doesn't it?"

But Fiona wasn't going to be caught the same way twice. "I wouldn't know. I don't think Alexander's capable of jealousy. Sometimes I wonder if he'd even notice if I was up to anything."

"Ever tempted . . . ?" asked Mrs. Pargeter mischievously.

"Huh. Chance'd be a fine thing." But it wasn't said with any meaning. It was just conventional banter. There was at the heart of Fiona Burchfield-Brown a kind of hopelessness, a lack of confidence that simply wouldn't believe that any man could ever show any interest in her. No, she had long since reconciled herself to always being with Alexander—and all that that entailed.

"Anyway, this man was asking about Theresa's visitors . . . ?" Time for another little lie. ". . . and I found this booklet thing around the house with a photograph of a bearded man in it, and I wondered whether you might have a look at it and see if you recognise him . . . ?"

"Oh, sure." Fiona Burchfield-Brown wiped her hand against her face as she had on their previous encounter. This time the streak she left was of silver polish rather than chicken grease. She looked at the proffered booklet.

"Yes. I'd say that was him. Pretty well certainly. I mean, he hadn't got that robe thingummy on."

"Dressed in scruffy clothes, you said . . . ?"

"Yes, and sort of out of date. Patterned shirt, jeans with a bit of a flare, trainers . . ."

It sounded as though it had been Brother Brian. The

clothes would fit in with the Church of Utter Simplicity's ostentatious unworldliness.

"Well, thank you. That's a great help, Fiona. And now if this bloke rings again, I'll be able to tell him. And finally get him off my back, I hope."

"Good luck. I jolly well hope you do."

It really did feel cold as Mrs. Pargeter left Fiona's front door. She clutched the Church of Utter Simplicity booklets to her ample mink-clad bosom to ward off the chill.

Jane Watson, Mrs. Nervy the Neurotic, was walking briskly along the pavement from "Hibiscus." At the gate of "High Bushes" their paths crossed.

Mrs. Pargeter was determined to make contact with the one Smithy's Loam wife she had not yet met. "Good morning," she said cheerily.

Jane Watson jumped as if a gun had been fired behind her ear. She flashed a furtive look at Mrs. Pargeter.

What happened then was very odd. The expression of shock in Jane Watson's eyes changed in a second to a look of sheer, blind panic. Without saying a word, she turned her head sharply away and rushed off down the road so fast she was almost running.

The incident made Mrs. Pargeter all the more determined to make contact with the frightened woman. There was something very odd going on there. Something that required explanation.

CHAPTER TWENTY-ONE

~~~~~~

Mrs. Pargeter sat in the back of the chauffeur-driven limousine on the way to Bedford and tried to still the growing
anxiety within her. She was not a woman prone to panic.
Her temperament was naturally equable, and the years of
her marriage to the late Mr. Pargeter, a marriage whose
excitements might have aggravated any tendency towards
nervousness in some wives, had in her case simply taught
her the values of patience and control. Though, of course,
she had had her anxious moments when her husband was
away on particularly important business trips, she had always disciplined herself into keeping the nature of the risks
he undertook in proportion.

But the anxiety she was now feeling about Theresa Cotton continued to grow, in spite of the rigid constraints of logic she imposed on it.

The former resident of her house had not left it in the conventional way, of that Mrs. Pargeter felt increasingly certain. Theresa Cotton had set up an elaborate subterfuge about her departure, she had devised a scenario specifically to mislead her neighbours, but that scenario had not been followed. Something had happened to change her plans.

And Mrs. Pargeter didn't think that that something had been a simple change of mind. No, her conjectures were more ominous.

One of these conjectures, though, could be checked out comparatively easily.

Which was why she was travelling to Bedford.

"Oh, do come in. He's just upstairs changing."

The woman at the door was modest, but comfortable-looking. So was the house she ushered Mrs. Pargeter into.

"We moved up here when he started. You know, ten years is a long time. Thought it'd be easier if we were on the spot."

"Of course. How much longer has he got to go?"

"Another five. Just half-way. Mind you, could be a lot less with good behaviour. And his behaviour's been perfect. So I'm hoping we'll see him out in a year . . . eighteen months."

"Good. I do hope so."

"Come through into the sitting-room. Don't mind Baby, will you?"

Mrs. Pargeter went into the room indicated. It was full of the evidence of a young family. A cheerfully cooing, drooling baby rocked itself back and forth in a sprung chair. A boy of three and an eighteen-month-old of indeterminate sex were on the floor, absorbed in some elaborate game with toy cars and cereal boxes, and hardly looked up at the newcomer.

"Do take a seat, please." Mrs. Crabbe smiled expansively at her visitor. "Would you like a cup of tea? Or coffee? Whichever you like."

"Coffee'd be lovely."

"That's what he'll want, and all. He says the coffee inside tastes like metal polish."

The homely Mrs. Crabbe went off to the kitchen, leaving Mrs. Pargeter to observe the charming domestic scene. It was one of peaceful chaos. The warm, comforting chaos that is inevitable in any household containing three children under four. An ordinary domestic scene.

Perfectly ordinary. In fact, the only thing that made it extraordinary was that the man of the house had been in Bedford prison for the past five years.

At that moment the man in question appeared. He was casually dressed in a cardigan, cord trousers and bedroom slippers. Just like any other husband and father taking it easy in his own home. Only the aggressive shortness of his hair suggested that he might have a life outside (or perhaps "inside" would be more accurate).

His welcome was as warm as his wife's had been. He clasped Mrs. Pargeter's hand in both of his. "Hello! Great pleasure to meet you at last. I've heard so much about you. Quite honestly, Mr. Pargeter—I mean, the late Mr. Pargeter—goodness, the amount he used to talk about you. On about you all the time, he was."

"Really? I didn't know that."

"Certainly. All the time."

"What, even when you were working?"

"Particularly when we was working. Goodness, your ears must've been burning all the time he was away. A pearl among women, he called you. A pearl among women."

"Oh . . ." Mrs. Pargeter blushed charmingly.

"And now I have the pleasure of meeting you, I can see he was dead right."

"Thank you." Mrs. Pargeter decided it was time to reciprocate the odd compliment. "You've got yourself very nicely set up here."

He shrugged dismissively. "Well, all right to tide us over. I mean, when I'm, er . . . when I'm my own master again, I'll move us somewhere that's more our style. But this is all right, you know, while the kids is little. Bit of a squash when they get much bigger, though."

"It's fine. And very convenient."

"Yes."

"You know, for visiting . . ."

"Oh, sure. Yes, well, I get out as often as I·can." The eighteen-month-old tottered across and nuzzled at his or her father's knee. The silky hair was affectionately rumpled. "I mean, obviously sometimes it's tricky, but I think, by and large, I probably see as much of the kids as most fathers . . . certainly more than those who leave for work before the little 'uns wake up and get back after they've gone to bed."

He could have been describing the fathers of Smithy's Loam, Mrs. Pargeter thought.

"I mean, what kind of communication do they get with their nippers, I ask you, only seeing them weekends when Dad's probably tired out and bad-tempered?"

"Not much, I would imagine."

"No. Well, I'm all in favour of the family unit. I think, if more families stuck together—even when things get difficult—there'd be less crime in this country of ours."

"I think you're right."

"If kids aren't brought up with any standards in the home, then how on earth can anyone expect them to know right from wrong when they grow up?"

"Exactly."

"Now, I don't go along with everything this government stands for, but—"

However, this encomium of Victorian values was interrupted by the return of Mrs. Crabbe with the coffee. As she bent down to put the tray on a low table, her husband gave her rump an affectionate pat. She poured the coffee. It was delicious, fresh-roasted, strong, a million miles away from the "metal polish" served in Bedford prison.

"All right, love," he said, when the coffee was poured and sugary biscuits had been distributed. "Business."

His wife nodded obediently and started for the kitchen. "Shall I take the kids?"

"If you wouldn't mind, love. I know they're young, but what they don't know, they can't tell no one about." He smiled at Mrs. Pargeter. "As your late husband always used to say."

"Yes. One of his mottoes, that was."

The baby was carried out, and the older two lured away cheerfully enough with promises of crisps and drinks. Mrs. Crabbe closed the sitting-room door and her husband turned to his visitor.

"Right. What can I do you for?"

"Well, I hope you don't mind, but—"

"Of course I don't mind. Anything you need, lady, you just say the word. Quite honestly, your late husband done so much for me, I could never repay it if I tried for a million years, so you just ask away."

Mrs. Pargeter settled into her armchair. "All right, listen. I need a kind of . . . burglary done and my late husband always said—I mean, not that he ever talked to me about his work—but he made it clear to me that, when it came to getting in and out of places, there was no one in the world to touch Keyhole Crabbe."

Her listener nodded. No point in false modesty; she was saying no more than the truth.

"Well, anyway, Keyhole, what I need doing is a bit delicate, and so I thought I'd ask your advice . . ."

"Very sensible. You come to the right place."

"I mean, I realise that . . ." She trod delicately. ". . . it's a bit difficult for you yourself at the moment . . . you know, your movements are a little restricted, but I wondered if you could recommend someone who might possibly—"

"Don't you count me out, lady. I'm sure I could do the job myself . . . I mean, depending where it is . . ."

"Well, that could be a problem. It's near Worcester . . ."

"Oh, easy. Do there and back inside the day."

"Yes, but I've a feeling this is going to have to be done at night."

"Ah." He hesitated for a moment, chewing his lip. "Nights are a bit trickier, certainly. They do have this unfortunate habit in nicks of shutting you up for the night. I don't mean I can't get out, obviously, but I try not to do it too often. Keep it for special occasions, you know, wedding anniversaries and suchlike. No need to take unnecessary risks, is there? Hmm . . ." He pondered for a moment, then made up his mind. "Oh, but, Mrs. Pargeter, for you . . . no, I'd have to do it myself."

"Not if it's going to be risky for you—"

"Don't even give it a thought. No problem. I got the routine sorted out. Sunday nights tend to be good, anyway, screws all dozy after a skinful on Saturday. No, Mrs. Pargeter, I couldn't stand the idea of no one else doing it for you. Hate to think of you being let down by some beginner. No, like you say, when it comes to anything with locks or keys, I am the best in the business. What's more, I never get caught."

Mrs. Pargeter could not prevent herself from looking a little quizzical, but Keyhole Crabbe quickly explained away his current situation. "Shopped, I was this time. Some silly little bugger—pardon my French—thought he could clean up my end of the market if I was out of the way." He laughed at the incongruity of the idea.

"And . . . what happened to him?" Mrs. Pargeter asked cautiously.

"Let's say he wasn't successful."

"Oh dear."

"No, don't get me wrong, lady. No violence. I hate violence. Never done anyone no good, hitting people. Not from Cain and Abel onwards. No, I done a straight tit-for-tat on this young chancer. Got him shopped, and all. He's in an Open Prison. Ford, you know, down near Bognor. And he can't even get out of *there*. Which goes to show exactly how good he is, dunnit?" he concluded with satisfaction.

Mrs. Pargeter smiled. She liked Keyhole Crabbe, and she appreciated his values. They coincided almost exactly with her own.

"Anyway," he said, offering her the biscuits again, "give me a bit more gen on this job you want done . . ."

CHAPTER TWENTY-TWO

"I don't know, Theresa seemed sort of anonymous," said Sue Curle after some deliberation. "I mean, obviously I knew her, and one sort of went through the motions socially, but it was as if there was something missing in the middle. I mean, I never felt that I got through to her."

"Did you feel the same, Vivvi?" asked Mrs. Pargeter.

"Yes, I suppose I did in a way." Vivvi Sprake wrinkled her nose up cautiously. "There was something sort of . . . shut-off about her. I mean, she was perfectly friendly, and very helpful—she fed our cat while we were away in Portugal, and I watered her plants when they were off, that sort of thing—but I don't know, she seemed to be sort of distancing herself all the time."

"And was that the same when her husband was around?

I mean, did it make any difference when he went up North?"

"Don't think it made any difference at all," said Vivvi. "Theresa was always like that."

But she had replied too quickly. Again, Mrs. Pargeter was aware of an unusual reaction from Vivvi when the name of Rod Cotton came up. There was something there to be probed further. When the right opportunity arose.

Mrs. Pargeter was pleased with the little impromptu coffee party she had arranged. Only Vivvi and Sue. All the other Smithy's Loam second cars had been out that Monday morning when the idea came to her, but Vivvi and Sue had been so surprised by the sudden invitation that neither had had time to make up excuses. If excuses were required. Probably not, Mrs. Pargeter surmised. Both women would be sufficiently intrigued to see how she had changed the interior of the Cottons' house to come across the road, anyway.

"What impression did you get, Sue?" she asked, moving the heat away from Vivvi for the time being. "Do you think Theresa had a weak personality?"

"No, not really. She just seemed to be very self-suffi-cient, you know, like there was an inner core of her that was completely private and that no one could touch."

"Hm. And she never gave the impression that she was dissatisfied with her life here?"

"Dissatisfied with her life in Smithy's Loam?" asked Sue Curle, struck by the incongruity of the idea. "No, why should she be? I mean, she had a husband who was earning a packet. More than that," she added bitterly, "she had a husband who didn't keep putting his hand up every skirt he came across."

Mrs. Pargeter flashed a look at Vivvi Sprake. Yes, there

was some reaction. Quickly concealed, but it had been there. What had happened between Rod and Vivvi?

"And did Theresa ever have a job herself?" she asked diffidently, still trying to find a way into the secret life of the missing woman.

"I think she did before they were married," said Vivvi, "but Rod was old-fashioned about that. Thought it reflected badly on him for his wife to have to go out to work. Anyway, he was coining it, so there wasn't much point. Anything she earned'd only add to his tax bill."

That put women's independence in its place, thought Mrs. Pargeter. She tried a new approach. "But you don't think Theresa ever wanted anything different? Anything more spiritual? Did she ever talk about values? Or materialism?"

"What is this?" Sue Curle laughed easily. "Honestly, Mrs. Pargeter, it sounds like you're filling out some questionnaire."

"Sorry. Just a nosy old woman," she covered up quickly. "It's just . . . I'm sorry, one does get sort of interested in the people who've lived in a house before you."

Both Sue and Vivvi looked blank at this idea. Clearly they had no interest in the people who had owned their houses before them. Once their financial and social status had been established, former owners ceased to have any relevance. The residents of Smithy's Loam continued to move in their own selfish circles.

Still, neither of them commented on their new neighbour's eccentricity. "Actually," Sue went off on a new tack, "the reason I thought of questionnaires was that I had some market researcher round this morning . . ."

"Oh, so did I," said Vivvi. "Woman with a Welsh accent . . . ?"

"That's right. Asking about marital status and that sort of thing. I was able to air some of my views on the subject of men and divorce." Sue smiled grimly. "Seemed quite a sensible woman, I thought."

Mrs. Pargeter took in this information with quiet satisfaction. She felt fairly certain that the Welsh "market researcher" was Truffler Mason's assistant. Sue Curle's commendation of the woman's views on men and divorce seemed a sufficient pointer.

So that was good. It meant that Truffler's investigations were proceeding. In tracking down the Cottons, he would have to make enquiries in Smithy's Loam and market research was as good a cover as any other. It was also likely that his investigations would incidentally be finding out a few details about the other residents of the close. And such information could be very useful to Mrs. Pargeter later in her enquiries.

The only thing wrong was that the Welsh girl should have come to her door, too. Missing her out because she was the instigator of the enquiry was the kind of lapse that could give rise to suspicion. Mrs. Pargeter made a mental note to mention this to Truffler when they next spoke.

Although Sue had now drawn attention to her questionnaire approach, Mrs. Pargeter saw no reason to discontinue it. Why not keep up the image of a nosy old bat?

"When did you last see Theresa, Sue?"

"Hm?"

"Well, Vivvi, you said she came round to see you early evening of the night she left. And I know she went to see Fiona Burchfield-Brown, too. So I was wondering whether she did a complete circuit of Smithy's Loam, saying goodbye . . ."

"Oh . . ." Sue Curle looked suddenly confused, perhaps even embarrassed. "I'm not sure . . ."

"It would have been the Monday evening, between six and sevenish. Last Monday. But perhaps you were still at the office . . . ?"

"No," said Sue hastily. "No, I was back. Now I remember, yes. Kirsten had to go up to London to some club or other. She was leaving about five, and I had to get back from the office early. That's right, Theresa did just come round briefly to say goodbye."

"Just 'goodbye' . . . ?"

That question got a firm "Yes." Mrs. Pargeter wondered . . . Something odd there, too . . . So many crosscurrents in Smithy's Loam. So many hints that needed picking up. So many half-statements that needed completing. So many details that cried out for investigation.

Still, she must move slowly. As usual, she felt it would be a "softly, softly" approach that paid off in the end.

"It's strange," she mused casually, "how I keep thinking about Theresa Cotton . . . I mean, as you say, she didn't seem to have a strong personality at all, and yet I can sort of feel her presence around the house . . ."

She had floated this just to see what kind of reaction it would provoke, but all she got was more bitterness from Sue Curle. "She may well have had a very strong personality, who can say? But being stuck at home looking after a house for a husband is not the best way of demonstrating one's personality, is it? But that's the lot of the average woman, even now. Yes, even after all the publicity about Women's Lib and all the great things it's supposed to have achieved, the average woman is still stuck at home, totally eclipsed by her bloody husband."

"Oh, I wouldn't say—"

"It's true. Might as well be dead as stuck at home in the 'mere wife' role. God, life's bloody unfair. Get born with a tassel and you've got an advantage for the rest of your life."

"I don't think that's always true," Mrs. Pargeter protested. "I mean, in some relationships, the sexes are completely equal." That had been the experience of her marriage to the late Mr. Pargeter. But then of course she knew she had been exceptionally lucky.

Sue Curle poured scorn on this idea. "Huh. I'm sorry, Mrs. Pargeter, but it's a generation thing. You only say that because your generation was brainwashed into thinking that a girl's main aim in life was to get a husband, and once she'd got one she should spend the rest of her days kowtowing to the selfish bastard!"

Under normal circumstances, Mrs. Pargeter would have contested this extravagant generalisation, but she didn't want to deflect the conversation. She was fishing for information and knew that her best catch would come in unguarded statements from her two guests. So she contented herself with a "Well, maybe you're right."

"Of course I am," Sue Curle asserted. "God, what I'd give to have my time over again! Certainly I'd never get married. Never give any man power over me, oh no. Maybe I'd try exercising a bit of power over them."

"But I thought you said," objected Mrs. Pargeter reasonably enough, "that the power came with the tassel, as it were. I thought you said the men had always got the advantage."

"Oh, they think they have, but that's just a product of another form of brainwashing. You see, even for my generation, marriage and fidelity were still the ideals. But some of the young ones now just don't think that way."

"I thought this dreadful AIDS business was bringing monogamy back."

"I don't think it's making that lot change their behaviour much. Anyway, Mrs. Pargeter, I'm not just talking about sex. The young are much more prepared to be selfish, just to have a good time, than we ever were. I mean, take Kirsten . . ."

"Your *au pair*?"

"Yes, her life is completely dedicated to pleasure. She goes out with men if she chooses to, but ensures that they pay for everything. And she spends the rest of her time buying clothes or going to clubs or sending off endless bulky letters to friends in Norway."

"I thought she was over here to be helping you and learning the language."

Sue Curle tossed her head back. "Huh. And huh again. In fact, huh on both counts. She's useless. It's like having another child around. I have to go around tidying up after her. She won't even pick up a pair of her own dirty tights."

"Well, can't you get rid of her?"

"Oh yes, sure, I could. But, honestly, it's hardly worth it. For a start, I haven't got time to traipse round looking for a replacement at the moment. And, anyway, she goes back to Norway for good in a couple of months. I'm just hoping that between now and then I'll be able to sort something out. The trouble is, having just gone back to work, time is at a premium."

This thought prompted her to look at her watch, but before she could say it was time to be off, Mrs. Pargeter asked, "Where does Kirsten get the money to buy all these clothes? I didn't think *au pairs* were paid that much . . ."

"No, they're not. Must have rich parents, I suppose." Then she looked again at her watch. "Sorry, I must be off now. I've got to be in the office this afternoon, and I haven't sorted out anything for the kids' supper yet."

"Doesn't Kirsten even do that?"

This was greeted with another "Huh." Sue went on, "I don't know why people go on having *au pairs*. All I hear from my friends is a long history of disasters. Anorexia, pregnancies, drugs, boyfriends—ugh! I don't think I've heard of anyone who's had a happy experience with an *au pair*."

"I have heard," said Mrs. Pargeter mischievously, "of one or two husbands who have."

Sue Curle grinned wryly. "Yes. Right. That just about says it all, doesn't it? Another triumph for the tassel." She picked up her handbag. "Look, I must be off. Thanks very much for the coffee. It was a really nice break."

"I should be going, too," Vivvi Sprake agreed, perhaps too quickly, after Sue had disappeared up the front path. She didn't seem to want to be left alone with her hostess.

"Oh, I'm sure you don't have to rush, Vivvi. I did just want to ask you about something . . ."

"Oh. What?"

For a moment Mrs. Pargeter was thrown. Then she remembered her good old stand-by excuse. "About gardeners . . ."

Yes, about gardeners first. And then about Rod Cotton . . .

"Oh. All right." Vivi put her handbag down. She didn't look very happy about it, but she knew she couldn't rush off without actual rudeness.

"Yes, Vivvi. What I wanted to ask was—"

But then the telephone rang. Just at the wrong moment. It let Vivvi Sprake off the hook. As Mrs. Pargeter went to answer it, her guest said hastily, "Look, sorry, I really must dash. Didn't realise it was so late. We'll talk about gardeners another time—OK?"

And she was out of the front door before Mrs. Pargeter had picked up the receiver.

How infuriating!

"Hello?" said Mrs. Pargeter into the phone.

"Mrs. Pargeter? It's Keyhole." His voice was tense and subdued.

"Oh?"

"I did it last night. Like you asked."

"Oh yes?"

"And I'm afraid you was right."

"Oh dear," said Mrs. Pargeter, reaching for a chair to support herself. "Oh dear, oh dear."

CHAPTER TWENTY-THREE

"Tell me what happened, Keyhole," she said.

"Job went easy. No problem. Sorted things out in the nick . . ."

"Wasn't that difficult?"

"No. Like I said, done it before. You know, wedding anniversaries, that kind of special occasion . . ."

"Yes."

"Mind you, of course, any celebrations have to be on the, sort of, domestic side. Can't really take the missus out for a nice meal, or up West for a show, you know, bit risky, that."

"I'm sure. But, last night . . ."

"Oh yeah. Right. Last night. Well, as I say, no problem getting out of the nick. In many ways it's easier, really, doing it after we've all been locked in. Screws aren't looking out for trouble. They, like, relax their vigilance. I mean, during the day they—"

"Yes."

The tension in Mrs. Pargeter's voice got through to him, and Keyhole Crabbe speeded up his narrative. "Anyway, outside the prison, met up with my mate all right. He'd got the car and organised the gear, skeleton keys and that, and off we go to Worcester. No problem finding the place. We done our homework and knew exactly where to go. Blooming great warehouse, it was."

"What was the security like?"

"Nothing to worry about."

"You mean there wasn't any?"

"Oh no. They got a couple of blokes with dogs come round, you know, patrol every hour or so. And they got these alarms on the doors and windows. But my mate's sussed it all out beforehand, so we don't have no difficulty."

"And no problem getting into the depository?"

"No. Three locks, all dead easy. Could've done them with a piece of soggy macaroni."

"And inside?"

"Bloody big, I'll say that—pardon my French. All these blooming great containers. That could've been a problem . . . you know, so many of them . . . not knowing where to look, that sort of number. Could've spent a long time going through everything in a big place like that. Heavy gear to move, and all."

"But you managed?" Mrs. Pargeter urged him on.

"Yes. Like I say, my mate's good. He'd done his research on the inside of the place, too. Took me straight to the right container."

"So you started to unpack it?"

"Yeah. Glad there was two of us. Half weigh a lot, wardrobes and that."

"Yes?" Mrs. Pargeter was finding the tension unbearable. "So where was it? What did you find?"

"You was right. It was in the freezer."

"Oh."

"That was locked, and all. No problem there, though . . ." He seemed to be slowing down again, unwilling to continue with his story.

"Come on, Keyhole. Tell me what you found."

His voice was thick and low as he continued. "We open the freezer. There's this something wrapped in polythene . . . Heavy. We pull it out. We unwrap it. And yes, it's a body."

"I'm sorry," Mrs. Pargeter murmured. "I'm very sorry to have put you through that."

"Don't worry. You had warned me, tipped me the wink, like. Not as if it was a complete surprise." He swallowed noisily down the line. "Nasty, though."

"Yes. And I suppose, having been in there more than a week . . ."

"Wasn't too bad from that point of view, Mrs. Pargeter, actually. Tightly wrapped in the polythene, good seal on the freezer lid, wasn't in too bad a state."

"Good." Mrs. Pargeter hesitated, unwilling to have her next, inevitable question answered. No way round it, though—had to be asked. "And who was it, Keyhole . . . ?"

"A woman. About forty. Fully clothed. Red hair."

Poor Theresa Cotton. Now the anxieties and uncomfortable speculations of the last few days had been proved real, Mrs. Pargeter felt weak and drained. Tears, she knew, were not far away. Tears for a woman she had only met a couple of times, but whose murder seemed to dispossess her more than the deaths of friends who had been much closer.

"Tell me, Keyhole," she murmured. "Was there anything else in the polythene? Or in the freezer?"

"All we found was a tie. Man's tie. Some school's Old Boys . . . cricket club . . . something like that, anyway. That was what did it."

"She was strangled?"

"Yes."

"Any other wounds on her?"

"Not that we could see. No blood on her clothes, nothing like that."

"No." That at least suggested that the attack had been a surprise. A quick death. Mrs. Pargeter tried to comfort herself with the thought.

"So what did you do, Keyhole?"

"Like you said, Mrs. Pargeter. Wrapped the body up, just as it had been. Back in the freezer. Freezer back in the container. All the rest of the furniture put exactly where we'd moved it from. No one'll know we been in there."

"And there's no danger that any fingerprints or . . . ?"

"Mrs. Pargeter . . ." he said, aggrieved and offended.

She covered the gaffe as quickly as she could. "I'm so sorry, Keyhole. Wasn't thinking."

"No." He sounded only partly mollified. "Look, Mrs. Pargeter, I'm going to have to ring off soon . . ."

"Why? Where are you phoning from?"

"The Governor's office. About the only decent direct-dial line out in this place."

"What, you've made yourself a key . . . ?"

"Of course. Well, I like to ring home every couple of days, see how the kids is getting on."

"Yes."

"But, anyway, the Governor's doing an inspection and he'll be back any minute, so I'd better scarper sharpish."

"Mm. Well, look, Keyhole, I can't thank you enough for—" A sudden thought stopped her in mid-sentence.

"Keyhole, one thing . . ."

"Yeah?"

"You're sure there wasn't any money in the freezer? Or in the polythene wrapping?"

"What, you mean coins or—?"

"No, notes. A lot of notes."

"Not a sign. Nothing. Like I say, nothing but the body and the tie."

So, although Theresa Cotton had been found, over two thousand pounds was still missing. Murders had been committed for much less, Mrs. Pargeter reflected. Even in affluent surroundings like Smithy's Loam.

"Look, Keyhole, I'm eternally in your debt for—"

"Gotta scarper!" she heard, before the phone was slammed down.

She had a momentary pang. She had got Keyhole Crabbe into this. If he were caught in the Governor's office, all kinds of unpleasant details about his escapological feats might come to light. He could even lose his remission for good behaviour. She thought tenderly of the sweet domestic scene she had witnessed so recently in Bedford.

But the anxiety only lasted for a moment. She had confidence in Keyhole. He was far too canny an operator to get caught, unless someone shopped him again. No, Keyhole Crabbe would be all right.

Mrs. Pargeter stayed sitting by the phone in the hall. She still felt exhausted.

141

And she was in a dilemma as to what to do next.

She remembered her late husband's precepts about the police. What they did not know, generally speaking, they did not need to know. Ignorance in the Police Force, he had always maintained, was a natural state, and who are we, he would ask with a disarming shrug of his shoulders, to interfere with nature?

On the other hand, this was murder. And somehow murder changed the rules.

She went upstairs and found the address book which had proved so useful over the last weeks. The late Mr. Pargeter's listings had furnished her with a car-tracing service, a Missing Persons bureau and a lock specialist; she felt confident that it could also provide a police informer.

There was a selection to choose from. She rang the first number and, as ever, the magic of the late Mr. Pargeter's name worked instantly.

The man at the end of the phone took the details impassively. He asked no questions, simply agreed to make an anonymous call to the Worcestershire Constabulary, suggesting that they should inspect a certain container in a certain furniture depository.

Mrs. Pargeter put the phone down wearily. The wheels had been set in motion. Now it was only a matter of time before the police arrived in Smithy's Loam.

She went into the sitting-room. It was only lunch-time, but she felt in need of a drink.

But, as she entered the room, she shivered. This, she felt sure, was where Theresa Cotton had been strangled only a fortnight before.

But who by, that was the question. Who by?

CHAPTER TWENTY-FOUR

It didn't take long.

No, give the British police their due (and even the late Mr. Pargeter had recommended that they should be given their due—not a lot else, but certainly their due), once they had the tip-off, they acted quickly.

On the following day, the Tuesday, the one o'clock news carried a brief announcement about a woman's body having been found in a furniture warehouse near Worcester, and by late afternoon the police were round at Smithy's Loam.

They had had no problem in guessing the identity of the corpse. The records of Littlehaven's, the removal company, showed where the furniture had come from, and that was obviously the first place to investigate. It took the minimum of enquiry to find out that the freezer's owner

had been a red-haired woman of about forty. Formal iden-
tification would have to wait until next-of-kin had been
contacted (and Mrs. Pargeter reckoned there might be
problems contacting the most immediate next-of-kin), but
the police were pretty sure that they were investigating
the murder of Theresa Cotton.

It was inevitable that one of their first ports of call should
be the deceased's former home, which was probably also
the scene of her strangling. Mrs. Pargeter had reconciled
herself to this fact from the moment that she authorised
the tip-off, and patiently awaited the police's arrival.

Two plain-clothes men came at about four in an un-
marked car. Their inconspicuous arrival might delay the
news for an hour or so, but Mrs. Pargeter felt convinced
it would soon be all round the close.

She responded like the good citizen that she was, inviting
them in, offering them tea, bewildered as to what on earth
it could be that they had come to see her about. She gave
the ingenuous appearance of someone with nothing on her
conscience, into whose head the thought that their visit
might be related to some shortcoming of her own did not
even enter.

(Her performance in this role was totally convincing.
But then it was one which she had rehearsed quite frequently during her life with the late Mr. Pargeter.)

She was properly surprised and appalled when the police
told her the suspected identity of the corpse. Yes, she had
heard the item on the news, but it had never occurred to
her that there had been any connection with . . . Oh dear,
she felt dreadful . . . Mrs. Cotton had seemed such a
charming person, it was awful to think that she . . . Goodness, wasn't it a terrible world we all lived in . . .

As tactfully as they could, without actually announcing that they thought the murder had taken place in the room where they were sitting, the police said that they might have to bring in some experts to examine the house and surroundings.

Of course, murmured Mrs. Pargeter, still in shock, of course.

And would she mind answering a few questions about Mrs. Cotton, the presumably *late* Mrs. Cotton?

No, of course not, murmured Mrs. Pargeter, of course not. Though, it must be remembered, they had only met very briefly . . .

In her replies to the police's question, Mrs. Pargeter stuck undeviatingly to the late Mr. Pargeter's rule about telling the truth, and nothing but the truth, though not necessarily the whole truth.

She produced the Dunnington address that Theresa Cotton had given her, and said, truthfully enough, that she had tried to make contact about the central heating, but had been unable to obtain the number. She felt tempted to save the police a bit of time by telling them that the address was false, but was afraid that might raise too many questions about her interest in the case. Anyway, it wouldn't take them long to find it out for themselves.

No, she hadn't seen Mrs. Cotton during the actual change of ownership of the house. She explained how Theresa was to have moved out on the Monday, while she herself did not move in until the Wednesday.

She was asked if she had noticed anything unusual, or if anything unusual had been said by the vendor, during her pre-purchase inspections of the property, but Mrs. Pargeter was forced to answer—again strictly within the bounds of truth—"no" to both questions. It had, after all, been a very simple transaction. She herself had nowhere to sell, and apparently the Cottons had had no problems with their purchase (since they weren't buying anything, this was hardly surprising).

Then came a question that gave her a moment's indecision. Had she found anything in the house that the Cottons had left behind? Anything unexpected?

For a moment she vacillated about mentioning the letter to the Church of Utter Simplicity. Her finding it had been so serendipitous, she did feel a proprietary interest in the letter as her own private clue.

On the other hand, she did not wish to obstruct the police investigation unnecessarily. And she thought she had probably got as much as she was likely to get out of the Church of Utter Simplicity connection. Besides, the hypocritical atmosphere of the place had so repelled her that the idea of putting the wind up the members of the Church held a mischievous attraction. Although she did not think anything actually criminal (assuming that taking advantage of the gullible is not criminal) was happening there, she still doubted whether the foundation would welcome investigation. Mrs. Pargeter was not by nature a vindictive person, but she did relish the idea of that unattractive Brother Michael being discomfited.

So she produced the letter for the police. Yes, she had glanced through it, but it hadn't meant a lot to her. Seemed to go on rather about religion. No, she hadn't known that Mrs. Cotton was religious. As she had said before, it had been a very brief acquaintance.

At this point the policemen stopped their flow of questions and seemed to hesitate before embarking on a new course. Mrs. Pargeter had the feeling that what they were about to ask was the most important part of their enquiry.

Finally the question came. Had she had any dealings during the house purchase with *Mr.* Cotton?

No, she hadn't. He had been transferred up North and started the new job. That was why the house was being sold.

Mrs. Pargeter didn't see the point of telling the police that the new job was as much a work of fiction as the new address. Apart from avoiding questions about her own curiosity, she wanted to give them something to do for themselves, and she was sure that the discovery of the nonexistent job would give enormous satisfaction to some eager young detective. Pity to deprive him of his thrill.

The police asked more about Rod Cotton, but she couldn't help them. They'd never met, you see, and she hadn't really been in Smithy's Loam long enough to pick up any local gossip about him.

And no, she had no idea where he might be.

Oops! That was a bit of a lapse. She covered it up quickly. Well, that was to say, she didn't know where he was if he wasn't at home . . . But presumably they could contact him at the Dunnington address . . . couldn't they?

The two policemen thanked her for her helpfulness. They were afraid that there were almost bound to be more questions at a later date. And they hoped she would bear with the arrival of their forensic team to examine the house.

"Are you saying," asked Mrs. Pargeter in an awestruck voice which was only partly put on, "that you think the murder took place *here?*"

"It's a possibility we can't rule out," came the diplomatic reply.

"Oh dear. The trouble is, of course, that I'll have moved everything, won't I? I mean, the sort of clues you're looking for. You know, you do when you move into a new house, don't you? You move stuff around, and you sweep and tidy and Hoover and . . ."

"Yes, I agree, Mrs. Pargeter. They may not find much, but such examinations do have to be carried out."

"Of course."

"So, as I say, if you will bear with us . . . ?"

"No problem. Goodness, I'd do anything to help you find the person who's done this dreadful thing."

"Thank you very much, Mrs. Pargeter. I only wish more people in this country of ours were as cooperative and public-spirited as you are."

"Oh, don't mention it," said Mrs. Pargeter, with a slight simper.

The forensic team arrived soon after, and Mrs. Pargeter, cooperative and public-spirited as ever, kept out of their way while they dusted for fingerprints and checked carpets and furniture throughout the house.

Through the net curtains of her bedroom, she saw the two policemen moving in the twilight from house to house, questioning the other residents of Smithy's Loam.

And, predictably, not long after the police, the press arrived in droves. Mrs. Pargeter was able to use the excuse of the forensic team's presence not to let them in, but they tried all the other houses in the close.

The varying receptions they met with were indicative of the characters of the residents. Fiona Burchfield-Brown, all bumbling good nature, invited them in. Vivvi Sprake was also welcoming, eager to talk, while Kirsten at "Perigord" (her employer must still have been at the office) seemed to see their arrival as an opportunity for her to achieve international stardom. She stayed on the doorstep for some time, talking effusively, with many gestures, to anyone willing to listen.

Carole Temple, predictably, slammed the door in the reporters' faces.

And, though her car stood in the drive of "Hibiscus," and though there were lights on in the house, Jane Watson would not even come to the door.

Mrs. Pargeter sat on her bed gazing out over the lamplit circle of Smithy's Loam, and thought.

So . . . the first priority of the police was going to be to find Rod Cotton. Logical, really. In all marital murder cases, the most common criminal is the spouse. And, in this case, the murder weapon also pointed towards Theresa's husband.

Hmm . . . Mrs. Pargeter wondered whether the police would find it easier to trace the missing man than she had. At least, she thought with an inward grin, Truffler Mason was already out looking.

So she had a head start. And she had played fair with the police by giving them the letter to the Church of Utter Simplicity. Fair dos. Now they were starting on equal terms.

Because, however much she tried not to, Mrs. Pargeter couldn't help seeing the murder investigation as a kind of contest.

Mrs. Pargeter versus The Police.

And it would be a bold punter who would predict which of them was most likely to reach the solution first.

CHAPTER TWENTY-FIVE

~~~~~~

The Welsh voice answered. Mrs. Pargeter did not take it to task about missing her out of the "market research" survey. That was something to be raised discreetly at a later date with the voice's employer.

"Is Mr. Mason there?"

"I'm sorry. He's out on an investigation. Can I take a message?"

"No, there's no—oh yes, well, you could actually. It's Mrs. Pargeter calling."

"Good morning."

"Good morning. Yes, I'd be grateful if you could pass on the message to Mr. Mason that there's no longer any need to look for the woman. It's just the man we need to track down now."

"Always bloody is, isn't it?" said the Welsh voice, predictably enough.

It occurred to Mrs. Pargeter that, though she had given the where-can-I-find-a-decent-gardener excuse a couple of airings, she hadn't yet used it on her immediate neighbour. They had talked of gardening, but not of gardeners. And she had a feeling that the dramatic news of Theresa's murder might make even the frosty Carole Temple relax a little into curiosity.

Her guess proved correct. When she knocked on the door of "Cromarty," its owner welcomed her with what, by Carole's somewhat narrow standards, probably amounted to fulsomeness. The visitor was instantly invited in for coffee. Living in a house where a murder had taken place did give a certain social cachet.

Mrs. Pargeter was sat down in the sitting-room, while Carole went off to make coffee. The room was immaculately furnished—if one's taste ran to louvred cupboard doors, beaten brass surrounds to log-effect fires, Capo del Monte figurines posing winsomely on top of dark veneered units, and curtains and chair covers with a frothing of frills on them.

It was aggressively clean and tidy. Mrs. Pargeter almost felt guilty for denting the cushions by sitting on them. A fantasy came into her mind of Carole Temple going round every hour on the hour removing individual specks of dust with a pair of tweezers, and of bashful motes deterred from entering the fanlight window by Carole's balefully hygienic stare.

The coffee cups and pot which her hostess brought in were sterile enough to be used in an intensive care unit. The biscuits had clearly been disciplined from birth not to shed crumbs, and the coffee-pot spout would not have dared to commit the solecism of dripping.

Carole Temple quickly dealt with the supposed reason for Mrs. Pargeter's visit. "I'm afraid I don't know any good gardeners. Or bad ones, come to that. We do everything ourselves. As I believe I once told you," she recollected with some asperity. "I think possibly the Sprakes have a gardener who comes in from time to time—you could ask them."

Yes, she would, Mrs. Pargeter decided. She and Vivvi had never got round to having their conversation about gardeners, had they? Surprising how durable that simple excuse was proving.

Carole Temple then moved on to the real reason for her sudden affability. "But, goodness me, poor Theresa! What a dreadful thing to happen in Smithy's Loam!"

"Or anywhere," Mrs. Pargeter observed mildly. She knew that its residents tended to see Smithy's Loam as the centre of the universe, but murder did remain a relatively offensive crime even in other parts of the world.

Carole Temple, stimulated by the news of murder, was prepared to be much less discreet than on their previous encounter. "Hmm," she ruminated knowingly. "I always thought there was something odd about that marriage . . ."

"Odd?" Mrs. Pargeter nudged gently.

"I mean, not on the surface. Theresa and Rod seemed . . . well, just like everyone else on the surface, but I had a feeling there were some pretty profound disagreements between them."

"Are you saying that you used to hear them quarrelling?"

"Good heavens, no." Carole Temple looked affronted that such a vulgar idea should even be mentioned in the context of Smithy's Loam. "No, I just sort of got this feeling that they didn't see eye to eye on everything."

"What, on materialism, for example?"

"I'm sorry?" Carole looked completely blank. "What do you mean?"

"Well, I'd sort of got the impression that maybe Theresa wasn't as keen on material things as her husband was."

"I'm afraid I don't understand."

"I mean that he was always wanting to buy things, keep up their standard of living, and Theresa wasn't even interested."

Carole Temple still looked bewildered. "But they didn't buy that much stuff. Well, only the sort of stuff one needs. If you're living somewhere like Smithy's Loam, you do have to maintain certain standards. I wouldn't have said they were particularly conspicuous consumers."

No. No more than their neighbours, anyway.

"And you never heard Theresa say she was dissatisfied with that kind of life?"

This idea, too, was incongruous to Carole. "No. Of course not."

So the spiritual emptiness of Theresa Cotton's life had, as Mrs. Pargeter suspected, remained her own secret. That fitted in with the furtiveness of her contacts with the Church of Utter Simplicity.

"Well, if it wasn't that kind of thing, Carole, what was it that was 'odd' about the Cottons' marriage?"

Faced with the direct question, Carole became coy and evasive. "Oh, I don't know. Just a sort of feeling I got. Well, I mean, their long separations, for a start . . . From the moment he went up North, so far as I know, Theresa made no effort to go up and join him—even for the odd weekend."

No, well, of course there were very good reasons why that hadn't happened, but Carole Temple couldn't be expected to know them.

"You think they were growing apart then, do you?"

"Reading between the lines, I'd say, yes."

"Hmm." Mrs. Pargeter nodded slowly. "Do you think there was any infidelity?"

Carole's face became cautiously knowing.

"On either side?" added Mrs. Pargeter.

"Well," said Carole Temple, condescending to share the great riches of her information, "let's say it wouldn't surprise me. Rod was away a lot, so presumably he had plenty of opportunities . . ."

"Yes, I suppose so." Mrs. Pargeter took a sip of her coffee and slowly put the cup down on its saucer. "And no rumours of anything nearer home . . . ?"

Her hostess became insufferably arch. "Once again, all I think I'd better say is that it would not surprise me . . ." Then, in response to Mrs. Pargeter's interrogative expression, she gave a little more. "No, it wouldn't surprise me at all to find that he'd made quite a close friendship *very* near to home. There was a week or so when he was between jobs—"

"Between jobs before he went up North?"

"That's right. And Theresa was out a lot at that time. But Rod had fairly regular weekday visits from someone else in Smithy's Loam." She let this hang in the air for a moment, before concluding, piously, "But I don't think it would be fair for me to say any more than that. Do you?"

Mrs. Pargeter thought it would be perfectly fair. In fact, she thought it was extremely unfair for her companion to hint so outrageously and then withhold the most important detail. But she wasn't optimistic about getting an actual name out of Carole.

"I suppose these things happen . . ." she said equably.

"Yes, yes, they do. I gather some women get very bored stuck in the house all day . . ." This was another idea apparently incomprehensible to Carole Temple. Clearly, stalking specks of dust with a pair of tweezers absorbed one hundred per cent of her own attention and enthusiasm. "I suppose they'll do anything for a change. And for someone that much younger, trapped in the house for most of the day with two children, maybe there's a kind of appeal about it . . ."

Mrs. Pargeter nodded. Yes; Vivvi Sprake was quite a bit younger than most of the other denizens of Smithy's Loam. Early thirties, while the rest were all safely over the forty mark. Their promised conversation about gardeners took on a new priority.

"Anyway, up to them, really, I'd say . . . wouldn't you?" Carole Temple shrugged righteously. "I mean, I'm the last one to spread gossip . . ."

Why was it, Mrs. Pargeter mused, that the only people who said they were the last ones to spread gossip were always such arrant gossip-mongers? It was a completely self-negating remark like "I'm the last one to make a fuss . . ." Fondly, she called to mind one of the late Mr. Pargeter's dicta: "Never believe a man who begins every sentence with 'Quite honestly'—-it's a sure sign he's lying."

She didn't think she was going to get much closer to the name of Rod Cotton's local bit of stuff, but having already identified the guilty party to her own satisfaction, she felt able to move the conversation forward.

"Do you think Theresa had any idea something was going on?"

"I would imagine so," Carole Temple replied tartly. "Didn't miss a lot, that one."

This was a new insight into Theresa Cotton's character. And considering how sketchy the image of the dead woman appeared to be amongst her neighbours, it was a very important insight.

"Are you saying that she was nosy?"

For the first time in their conversation, Carole Temple seemed to feel she had said too much, and started backtracking. "Oh, I think most people are naturally curious, don't you? Intrigued by what's going on around them. Just as we're all intrigued by having a murder case on our doorstep."

Mrs. Pargeter wasn't going to be shifted off her line of questioning quite so easily. "From what you said, you almost implied that Theresa Cotton used to spy on you . . . ?"

"No, of course not." Carole squashed this idea brusquely. "Well, if I gave that impression, I didn't mean to."

But the cover-up wasn't completely convincing. There had been some bad blood between the neighbours at some point, of that Mrs. Pargeter felt certain. And if Carole had thought Theresa over-curious, then maybe Theresa had seen something that her neighbour had not wished her to see . . .

And, if there had been some resentment or grudge between them, then it was just the kind of thing that Theresa would have tried to clear from her mind before dedicating herself to the Church of Utter Simplicity . . .

"Tell me, Carole . . ." said Mrs. Pargeter abruptly. "Did Theresa Cotton come to see you the Monday evening before she left—or was supposed to leave—Smithy's Loam?"

"What?" Carole Temple was thrown for a moment, but quickly regained control. "Oh, yes, she did. Just dropped in to say goodbye."

And what else, apart from goodbye, Mrs. Pargeter wondered. She looked fixedly at her neighbour and was rewarded by Carole's turning away to offer more coffee. Something had definitely happened, something had definitely been said that night. And Mrs. Pargeter felt confident that, given time, she could find out what had happened, and what had been said.

A pattern was beginning to emerge. A pattern of Theresa Cotton, following the recommendations of the odious Brother Michael, going round Smithy's Loam, clearing her mind of resentments and grudges. Fiona Burchfield-Brown had admitted that Theresa had appeared; so had Sue Curle, Vivvi Sprake, and now Carole Temple. Mrs. Pargeter wondered whether Jane Watson had been on the calling-list, too.

Each of the women Mrs. Pargeter had spoken to had said that the murder victim had come just to say goodbye. And yet each had spoken with some embarrassment. And, from the letter she had discovered, Mrs. Pargeter knew that the intention of Theresa's visits had been much more than just to say goodbye.

She became aware that Carole Temple was talking again. "It's tragic, isn't it, really? That people can do that kind of thing to each other?"

"Murder?"

"Mm. And to do it to someone you love—or at least to someone who presumably you did once love . . ."

" 'Yet each man kills the thing he loves,' " Mrs. Pargeter murmured,

> "By each let this be heard,
> Some do it with a bitter look,
> Some with a flattering word.
> The coward does it with a kiss,
> The brave man with a sword!"

Carole Temple looked at her in amazement. Evidently literary quotation was not part of the Temple lifestyle. Yes, suddenly Mrs. Pargeter noticed something she had missed about the spotless sitting-room—as in her own house during the Cottons' ownership, there were no books in evidence, no books of any sort, anywhere.

"*The Ballad of Reading Gaol*," she supplied helpfully. "My late husband was very fond of the works of Oscar Wilde."

It was true. The late Mr. Pargeter had found Wilde a great solace, especially in times of enforced idleness. *The Ballad of Reading Gaol* had been a particular favourite. That and *De Profundis*.

"Ah." Carole Temple remained nonplussed. "Still, as I say, it is tragic."

"Oh, indeed," Mrs. Pargeter agreed devoutly. "So . . . you think that Rod murdered Theresa?"

"Well, yes, of course. He was her husband." The matter-of-fact way in which this was said did not argue a very high opinion of the institution of marriage. "He must have done it. It's the only possible solution, isn't it?"

Well, no, thought Mrs. Pargeter to herself, there are one or two other possibilities.

CHAPTER TWENTY-SIX

"Mrs. Pargeter, it's Truffler," said the familiar bereaved voice. "I got your message."

"Oh, hello. Thank you for ringing back."

"I think I'd probably have worked out for myself that it was only the man you were after."

"Yes, I'm sorry. I was just afraid that, if you were actually out investigating, you might not have seen the papers or heard the news."

"No, I heard. Sad business, isn't it?" Since Truffler Mason made everything sound like a sad business, his intonation did not change for this observation.

"Yes. Very sad."

"Did you suspect that that was what had happened when you asked me to trace her?"

"I hoped it hadn't," Mrs. Pargeter replied cautiously, "but I was rather afraid it might have done."

Truffler Mason let out a mournful sigh. "Of course, it means that I'm not going to be the only one trying to find the husband . . ."

"No. The police are definitely on to him. They came and talked to me."

"Hm."

"Still, you've got a start on them."

"Oh yes," Truffler Mason agreed lugubriously. "Yes, a bit of a start, yes."

"Are you getting anywhere?" Mrs. Pargeter asked diffidently. She knew that Truffler worked at his own pace, and didn't want to appear to be nagging him.

"Yes, getting somewhere," he admitted dolefully. "Finding out a lot about his background—and a few other people's backgrounds. Haven't actually found him yet, of course—you'll know the minute that happens—but I've got a few leads."

"Have you, by any chance . . ." Mrs. Pargeter continued her cautious approach, ". . . found out where he went straight after leaving Smithy's Loam?"

"Well, after he was made redundant, he stayed around at home for a couple of weeks . . ."

"So I gather. Maintaining the myth that he was going on to this great new job in the North?"

"That's right."

"Any idea what he did while he was at home for that time?"

"No, not really. Drank a lot, I think."

And conducted his little affair with Vivvi Sprake, Mrs. Pargeter reckoned.

"Then he seems to have gone off to various places. I

haven't checked them all out yet. I'd really rather, if you don't mind, Mrs. Pargeter, give you all the details when I've completed the investigation."

"Yes, of course. I'm sorry, Truffler." She wanted to ask how long he thought that might be, but again didn't want to pressurise him.

Fortunately he anticipated her unspoken question. "I'm really moving along now, Mrs. Pargeter. Hope to have some information for you within the week."

"Thank you."

"I'm afraid," he went on, more dismal than ever, "it may be rather grim when we do find him."

Mrs. Pargeter was shocked. "You don't mean that we're going to find another corpse, do you?"

"Oh, no. Well, if we do, it won't be murder."

"Suicide?"

"I didn't say that." Truffler Mason was becoming uneasy. He didn't like discussing one of his investigations until it was all neatly sewn up and delivered. "What I'm saying is, everything I've found out about Rod Cotton suggests he's gone downhill."

"Downhill?" asked Mrs. Pargeter, eager to have the hint amplified.

But all Truffler Mason gave her was a gnomic "yes," and apologised once again that he'd really rather not say more for the moment.

So she was left to brood on the tantalisingly small amount of information he had given her.

Mrs. Pargeter decided that she needed another treat. All this investigation was very exhausting emotionally. Fortunately, in her researches into the area before she moved, she had compiled a comprehensive list of local restaurants, and it was—in a spirit of devilment—the most expensive of these that she rang to book herself a table for dinner.

The restaurant was in a pub just outside Dorking, though diners had a separate entrance from drinkers. Mrs. Pargeter enjoyed a leisurely vodka Campari in the bar, while she perused the menu, before selecting prawns in garlic and steak au poivre. She ordered a half-bottle of Vouvray to go with the starter, and of Crozes Hermitage for the main course.

From the restaurant bar, through a screen of wooden lattice-work, she could see into the pub, and it was with some shock that she recognised Sue Curle sitting in a private alcove of the saloon bar. Mrs. Pargeter was close to the lattice and had no fear that she herself could be seen.

Sue was not drinking alone. The man with her was a West Indian of strikingly good looks, dressed in a very smart light grey suit. Their hands were intertwined and they were talking with the urgent intensity of people who have either recently been in bed together or will soon be in bed together.

As Mrs. Pargeter looked on, Sue Curle glanced at her watch and reached suddenly across to touch her companion's cheek. They kissed intimately, then she rose to her feet and, with a furtive look to left and right, walked out of the pub without a backward glance.

Instinctively, Mrs. Pargeter looked at her watch. The handsome West Indian rationed out the remains of his glass of wine with slow slips, occasionally checking the time, then rose and, slinging his coat over his shoulder, walked jauntily out the same way.

Five minutes exactly by Mrs. Pargeter's watch. A familiar scenario. "We'd better not leave together—give me five minutes."

Hm, so Sue Curle's contempt for the male sex was not total.

Interesting . . .

She sat over her garlic prawns and Vouvray and thought about Theresa Cotton's murder. Or, more particularly, about the disposal of Theresa Cotton's body.

That was the odd element in the case. The strangling itself, given the lack of evident marks on the body, had been conducted with exemplary efficiency.

It was the placing of the body in the freezer that struck a discordant note.

True, the freezer had a lock, which would have prevented its falling open by mistake when being shifted by the removal men. But there remained an element of risk in the procedure. Might not the removal men have become suspicious because of the unusual weight of the freezer? Or when it arrived at the warehouse might not suspicions be raised that it hadn't been emptied properly and could contain perishable commodities (as indeed it did)?

Still, neither of these suspicions had arisen. In that sense, the murderer had succeeded. According to plan, the freezer had been stored away in its container, where it could have remained for some long time. As Keyhole Crabbe had said, the tightness of the polythene wrapping and the quality of the seal on the freezer lid had delayed decomposition and might well have contained the corpse's smell.

And maybe, Mrs. Pargeter reflected, the heaviness of the freezer wouldn't actually have raised suspicions. Since the storage of furniture was paid for according to bulk, it would have been a logical economy to fill a vacant space like an empty freezer with smaller items, and probably that was a practice to which the Littlehaven's men were accustomed.

But the fact remained that, even if the danger of immediate discovery was not great, the concealment of the body in the freezer could only be a temporary solution. Maybe not in the short term, but sooner or later, it was going to be discovered. And a murder enquiry, though delayed, would inevitably ensue.

Yes, the use of the freezer brought an air of improvisation into what was otherwise a well-planned murder.

Mrs. Pargeter tried to think what motives could drive someone to dispose of a body in that way.

It could be just the product of panic. Maybe the murderer had thought through the strangling, but not thought beyond the crime itself.

Alternatively, the murderer may have been content to buy time. For some reason, he or she only wanted the investigation delayed, confident that by the time the body was discovered, he or she would no longer be a suspect.

Or could it be even simpler than that? The murderer was so confident of not even being considered as a suspect that he or she made only a token attempt at disposing of the body. Maybe the murderer had such a solid alibi that the police would never crack it.

Or maybe there was such an obvious main suspect that the murderer had no fear of being investigated at all.

Back to Rod Cotton, thought Mrs. Pargeter. Truffler Mason had said that the dead woman's husband had gone downhill. When the police finally found him, his prospects might be even more downhill.

CHAPTER TWENTY-SEVEN

~~~~~~

On the night she died, Theresa Cotton was known to have visited four of the women living in Smithy's Loam. She had been to "High Bushes" to see Fiona Burchfield-Brown, to "Perigord" to see Sue Curle, to "Haymakers" to see Vivvi Sprake, and to "Cromarty" to see Carole Temple. Mrs. Pargeter would also have put money on the fact that Theresa Cotton had been to "Hibiscus" to see Jane Watson.

It was time, Mrs. Pargeter decided, that contact should be made with Mrs. Nervy the Neurotic. There must be some explanation for the woman's deeply anti-social attitude, and now that there was a murder to investigate, that explanation became rather important. Why was it that she behaved as if she were afraid of the other residents of Smithy's Loam? There had to be a reason other than mere shyness or arrogance.

Mrs. Pargeter knew that she would have to move carefully in establishing contact with Jane Watson. She had seen the woman cut people dead in the street, she had seen her refuse even to answer her door to the inquisitive pressmen. It was going to require some kind of trick to break through that impregnable defence.

The following morning the opportunity for just such a trick presented itself. Mrs. Pargeter received another visit from the police. The same two detectives returned and asked some supplementary questions, reverting time and again to the whereabouts of Rod Cotton.

Since Mrs. Pargeter had no information at all on this subject (and had no intention of putting them in touch with Truffler Mason, who might have had some), the conversation could not progress far. She was helpful and public-spirited, as ever, but couldn't really be of much assistance to their investigation.

Recognising this at last, the two detectives thanked her for her patience, apologised that they might well have to be in touch again, and crossed Smithy's Loam to "High Bushes," no doubt to address similar questions to Fiona Burchfield-Brown.

Some ten minutes later, observed by Mrs. Pargeter through her net curtains, the policemen moved on to "Perigord." Sue Curle must have been at the office, because the door was answered by Kirsten, smartly turned out in a new black and white striped dress. The detectives did not go in, and only talked briefly on the doorstep. Then, put off either by her ignorance or her fractured English, they left Kirsten, moving on to "Haymakers" and Vivvi Sprake.

They were there for about ten minutes, before reappearing to go and knock at the door of "Hibiscus." Jane Watson might have been able just to ignore the demands of the newspaper reporters, but she didn't dare do that with the police. The two detectives disappeared inside the house.

Mrs. Pargeter judged the timing to perfection. She let eight minutes elapse, before putting on one of her everyday minks, going out of her front door and walking briskly across to "Hibiscus."

She rang the bell and, as she had anticipated, Jane Watson came to the door. Behind her, just emerging from the sitting-room, were the figures of the two detectives, holding their hats, as if about to leave.

Good. Mrs. Pargeter congratulated herself on her timing. With the policemen as witnesses, she felt certain that Jane Watson would maintain at least the appearance of civility. She wouldn't want to unleash any unnecessary suspicions by suggesting dissensions among the residents of Smithy's Loam.

"Hello, I'm Mrs. Pargeter. We haven't really met properly, have we? I'm the one who's moved into the Cottons' house."

"Yes . . ." Jane Watson looked troubled and uncertain for a moment. Then she saw a let-out. "I'm sorry. The police are here, asking me some questions . . . you know, in connection with . . . what happened. Do you think it would be possible for you to call back another time . . . ?"

"No, it's no problem," said one of the detectives, spot on cue. "We'd just about finished. Don't let us interfere with your social life."

"Well . . . er . . ." Jane Watson looked confused. She didn't want to invite Mrs. Pargeter in, but equally she didn't want the detectives to see her turning her new neighbour away. She succumbed. "You'd better come in," she said, standing back with not very good grace.

"Thank you, dear." Mrs. Pargeter bustled into the house, looking very pleased with herself.

"May have to be in touch again, Mrs. Watson," one of the detectives apologised. "Sorry, as we were only just now saying to Mrs. Pargeter, these enquiries can take a hell of a long time."

"Yes. Yes, of course." Jane Watson looked weak and a little confused.

"Anyway, thank you so much for your assistance." The two detectives made their way off down the path.

Jane Watson closed the front door behind them and leant against it. With a defiant look at Mrs. Pargeter, she demanded, "Now what on earth do you want?"

The door to the sitting-room was still open. Uninvited, Mrs. Pargeter moved through it, saying, "Just a neighbourly call . . ."

Jane Watson followed her. "Look, what is this?"

There was anger in her voice, but not the confident anger of righteousness. It was the uncertain anger of anxiety.

Mrs. Pargeter looked at her. Jane Watson's looks were stuck in a time-warp. The Sixties. She looked like a bespectacled Mary of Peter, Paul and Mary; long blonde hair fading a bit now; pale eyes weak behind thick glasses; face, innocent of make-up, showing its lines. A marked contrast to most of the carefully coiffed and painted ladies of Smithy's Loam.

"It's just . . ." Mrs. Pargeter began, circling round to her subject, "really this murder that's made me come to see you. I mean, now we're all going through the same thing, all being questioned by the police and what-have-you, I thought we ought to stick together . . ."

"Why?" asked Jane Watson.

It was a disconcerting question—disconcerting chiefly because Mrs. Pargeter couldn't think of an answer to it.

"Well, I don't know," she replied accurately enough. "It's just strange for me, moving into a new house and then discovering that its former owner was murdered . . ."

Jane Watson grunted acknowledgement that that might be strange, but implied that the strangeness still did not explain Mrs. Pargeter's presence.

". . . and I was just wondering when you last saw Theresa Cotton . . . ?"

"The police asked that."

"Yes, and now I'm asking it."

"But the police at least have a reason for asking," said Jane with mounting anger. "It's their job. Whereas it's no business of yours at all."

"I'm just interested," said Mrs. Pargeter, with what she hoped was a disarming shrug.

It didn't disarm Jane Watson. "Everyone round here shows too much bloody interest in other people's lives! We all have a right to privacy, and that's something everyone should respect."

"Oh, certainly, certainly," Mrs. Pargeter agreed.

Jane Watson's eyes blazed. "Then why won't you respect mine!"

"All I want to know is whether Theresa Cotton came to say goodbye to you the evening before she died . . . ?"

Jane reacted sharply. "Why? What does it matter whether she did or not?"

"I just want to know," said Mrs. Pargeter simply.

A change came into the pale eyes behind their thick

lenses; they grew more cunning. "I do know why you want to know."

"Oh? Really?"

"Yes. I know you're connected with *them*."

"Them?" Mrs. Pargeter felt she was rather losing touch with the conversation, and what Jane Watson said next didn't dispel that impression.

"I know what they're like. Once they get their claws into you, they don't let go."

"What?"

"Theresa Cotton was one of them. And you're one of them."

Mrs. Pargeter began to fear for the woman's sanity, as these paranoid ramblings continued.

"And, oh yes, I admit it—I was one, too. But I escaped, I got away from it. And I'm never going to go back!" The cunning in the eyes was now giving way to a gleam of madness. "Oh, they think they can take everything from you, but they can't take your soul! No, that remains your own! They can't take away your self!"

Jane Watson was now very close. She took hold of Mrs. Pargeter's plump arms and gripped them tightly. "So you won't succeed, Mrs. Pargeter—or whatever your real name is! Theresa Cotton didn't succeed, either. She came round, trying to take me back, but I was too strong for her! And I'll be too strong for you, too!"

She certainly was strong. Her fingers were biting like metal into Mrs. Pargeter's flesh. They were hands that would have had no difficulty in strangling someone.

Mrs. Pargeter felt a tremor of fear. "I must go," she blurted out.

"Yes," Jane Watson hissed. "You shouldn't have come in the first place!"

With a final vindictive squeeze, she released her grip. Mrs. Pargeter scuttled out of the sitting-room towards the front door.

Jane Watson's words followed her. "And I hope now you won't try to come again! Theresa Cotton came to see me—yes, in answer to your question, she *did* come to see me. And look what happened to her!"

Mrs. Pargeter snatched open the front door, and burst out, breathless, into the relative calm of Smithy's Loam.

That woman, she thought, is mad.

CHAPTER TWENTY-EIGHT

The phone was ringing as Mrs. Pargeter entered the front door. She snatched it up and instantly recognised Truffler Mason's funereal tones.

"Listen, I've found him." Never had such exciting news been imparted in such an unexcited way. He sounded like a tiler giving an estimate for a roof repair.

"Rod? Where is he? Can I make contact with him?"

"Yes, you *can*," Truffler replied dubiously, "if you're sure you want to."

"You don't make it sound very attractive."

"It isn't very attractive. Do you really need to see him?"

She had no hesitation in saying "Yes." Mrs. Pargeter was now very determined that Theresa Cotton's murderer should be unmasked, and though of course she had great respect for the abilities of the police, she rather wondered whether they would be able to do it on their own. They didn't have the same kind of network of contacts as Truffler Mason; it might take them a very long time to trace the missing man.

And, though Mrs. Pargeter was by no means committed to the prevalent view that Rod Cotton had killed his wife, she knew that no investigation into the murder would be complete without an interview with the absent husband.

Truffler did not try to dissuade her. The late Mr. Pargeter, shortly before his death, had instructed the investigator to give any help his widow might require, and Truffler owed far too much to the late Mr. Pargeter to dream of disobeying those orders in the smallest particular.

He arranged with Mrs. Pargeter where they should meet early the next morning. "Oh, and don't dress too posh," he cautioned.

"What, not a mink or anything like that?"

"No. Goodness, no. Keep it simple. Don't want to be conspicuous."

"All right. If you say so. Anything special I should bring?"

"Some cash wouldn't be a bad idea. And a couple of half-bottles of whisky might come in," Truffler Mason concluded lugubriously.

Their rendezvous was outside the Embankment Underground station, but Mrs. Pargeter did not travel there by Tube. She was a bit old, she considered, to be traipsing around by public transport so early in the morning. So, mindful of the late Mr. Pargeter's constant advice that small economies only suited small minds, she had Gary's limousine deliver her.

But, with Truffler Mason's admonition about being inconspicuous freshly in her mind, she arranged for the car to deposit her outside the Sherlock Holmes pub in Northumberland Street, and walked down to the station.

She had dressed with care—and indeed with some difficulty. Her wardrobe did not boast a great many "inconspicuous" garments. The late Mr. Pargeter, during his lifetime, had always encouraged her to wear bright colours. Her beautiful complexion, he constantly maintained, could cope with them, and he liked to see her looking bright and cheerful in every sense when he returned from a business trip. So most of her dresses were in jubilantly coloured silks; her coats were selected from a small armoury of minks; and the ensembles were habitually complemented by a tasteful garnish of large jewellery.

For her encounter with Rod Cotton, she had, with some regret, relinquished all jewellery. She wore beige fur-lined boots, which not only kept out the chill rising from the pavements, but also concealed her silk stockings (she could never bring herself to wear any other kind). And she had forgone even her most humble and domestic mink, in favour of an old Burberry raincoat.

She missed the reassurance of the fur as she stepped briskly towards the Underground station. It was getting very wintry now. The edges of the pavements, not yet trodden away by early commuters, bore a salt-like crust of frost. As she passed their noisome cardboard fortresses under the railway arches, she felt a surge of pity for the newspaper-swaddled dossers who lay asleep on the cold pavements of London.

Truffler Mason was waiting for her. She had never seen him before in the flesh, but had no difficulty in knowing who he was. His great height and the long, sagging lines of his face—almost as if he had been made of candlewax and melted—fitted perfectly with the doleful voice.

"Play it whatever way you want," he said. "I'll come with you and talk to him if you need support."

"I think I'll probably be better off on my own," said Mrs. Pargeter with delicate tact. "Don't want to frighten him off or anything."

"OK, up to you. I'll stay in sight, though, just in case you need any help."

"Why should I need any help?" she asked innocently.

"Don't know how he's going to react to being approached, do you?"

"No, I suppose not."

"Nor how the others are going to react."

"Others?"

"Yes."

"What others?"

"Well, there are quite a lot of them, aren't there?"

"Quite a lot of who?" Mrs. Pargeter looked puzzled. "I'm sorry, Truffler, I'm not really with you . . ."

He pointed gloomily across the road. "Look, over there. That's where he is."

Mrs. Pargeter followed the line of his finger, and saw the row of human jetsam she had passed only moments before.

"You mean, the dossers . . . ? Rod Cotton is over there . . . with the dossers . . . ?"

Truffler Mason nodded. "Fourth one from the right."

"Good heavens," said Mrs. Pargeter.

The smell, a compound of old sweat, urine and stale alcohol, grew almost insupportably strong as she approached the line of padded bodies. The one that Truffler Mason, now protectively watching her from the other side of the road, had pointed out lay on top of three opened-out cardboard boxes. Under its coverlet of newspapers, the body was wrapped in an old greatcoat, once navy blue, but now faded to grey. From inside this, more newspaper, extra protection against the cold, spilled out. Stiffly-matted hair straying from under a woollen hat was all that could be seen of the head; its face was pushed into a pillow of a grubby padded carrier-bag.

The odorous cocoon gave no signs of life.

With caution, Mrs. Pargeter reached forward an elegantly booted foot and touched one of the stained trainers that emerged from the bottom of the greatcoat.

There was no reaction.

She tried again, this time giving the body's foot a firmer shove.

The third time, it worked. The pile of rags and newspaper twitched alive with remarkable speed. Suddenly it was sitting upright.

A haunted face glared at Mrs. Pargeter. It was lined with grime, circled by greasy hair and scrubby beard. The gummy eyes lurked suspiciously in deep recesses.

But, through the disguise of suffering and deprivation, it was undoubtedly the face that Mrs. Pargeter had seen in a photograph frame on the mantelpiece when she had first visited "Acapulco," Smithy's Loam.

The dosser was Rod Cotton.

CHAPTER TWENTY-NINE

"It's all right. I'll move on," said the dosser in instant reaction to his awakening.

His voice had not quite lost its educated origins, but had become slurred into a kind of anonymous, classless growl.

"I'm not moving you on," said Mrs. Pargeter. "I want to talk to you."

"Bloody do-gooders," the voice complained. "Why can't you leave us alone? Things are bad enough without you rubbing our bloody faces in it."

"I'm not a do-gooder. As I say, I just want to talk to you."

"Oh yes. Talk, talk, talk—maybe give me a cup of bloody awful soup—and then suddenly the talk'll get round to God, won't it? Well, don't bother. Just leave me to go back to sleep. God's irrelevant—got nothing to do with anything. If there was a God, he wouldn't let people end up like this, would he?" His right arm waved vaguely to encompass the other muffled bodies beside him. Mrs. Pargeter noticed that the wrist was enclosed in a grubby plaster cast. He turned his face away from her and buried it back into his carrier-bag pillow.

Mrs. Pargeter reached into her Burberry pocket. "I've got something for you."

"Don't want any of your bloody leaflets," the heap of clothes mumbled.

"I think you might want this." She turned the top, breaking the seal on one of the half-bottles of whisky.

The dosser turned instantly at this familiar sound and squinted up at her. She held out the open bottle towards him. With a quick look round to see that none of his neighbours were watching, he seized it and took a long swallow. Then another. And another.

Mrs. Pargeter held her hand out. "That's enough for the moment."

"No." He cradled the bottle to his chest.

She kept her hand outstretched. "Yes. You talk to me, you tell me what I want to know, and you can have the rest."

"I can have the rest now. I've got it," he said childishly, still clutching the bottle to him.

"Yes, you can have that," Mrs. Pargeter agreed, "but you can't have the second bottle."

"Second bottle?"

She half-lifted it out of her other Burberry pocket. The dosser took a long swig from the bottle he held and looked furtively thoughtful. "Why do you want to talk?"

"I just do." She lifted the second bottle fully out of her pocket and saw his eyes fix on it. "Come on, get up and talk."

He hesitated only for a moment, then shambled upright. He had difficulty straightening his body after its night on the cold pavement, and flinched with muscular pain as he pulled the packed newspaper out of his greatcoat. "Not talk here," he said cunningly. "Don't want the others to see."

He took another long, surreptitious swallow from his bottle, then, with elaborate precaution, hid it in his coat pocket. "Where d'you want to talk?"

"There's a café over there. Do you want to go in? I'll buy you some breakfast."

He grimaced. "Not food. Can't eat food early in the morning. Can't eat it much any time. Over-rated stuff, food."

"Shall we go through there?" Mrs. Pargeter pointed to the gates into Embankment Gardens.

He nodded. "You give me the other bottle?"

"When we've talked, yes."

She felt safer with him walking ahead of her. As he started off, she glanced across the road to Truffler Mason. She gestured with her head towards the gardens. He gave an almost imperceptible nod, and started moving in the same direction himself.

Mrs. Pargeter followed the malodorous figure ahead of her in disbelief. She knew Rod Cotton to be in his early forties, and yet the figure ahead shambled like something out of a geriatric ward. What could have happened in six months to reduce a resident of Smithy's Loam to this?

He hobbled to the nearest bench inside the gates, and slumped on to it. A smartly overcoated man with a bowler hat, already sitting there, registered the tramp's approach, and moved briskly away to the other end of the gardens.

Mrs. Pargeter sat down, as close to her quarry as her tolerance of his acrid smell allowed. He took the bottle out of his pocket, transferred it to his plastered hand and, again with a precautionary look around, unscrewed it and took another drink. Only about a quarter of the contents remained. He looked at her greedily. "The other bottle."

Mrs. Pargeter retained her cool. "When we've talked . . ." she said firmly, and then, timing it carefully, added the isolated monosyllable, ". . . Rod."

Only a flicker of recognition crossed his face. "Who's Rod?" he asked.

"You are."

"No."

"You are Rod Cotton."

He shook his head slowly, as if suddenly it had become very heavy. "No, I'm no one. I don't exist," he said, slurring more than ever.

"You are Rod Cotton," Mrs. Pargeter persisted. "I know you are."

A pathetic cunning came into his eyes. "Who was Rod Cotton?"

"Rod Cotton was a man in his early forties, married to Theresa, living at 'Acapulco,' Smithy's Loam. Until six months ago, he was a Sales Director with C, Q, F & S."

He gave a twisted smile. "I don't look like a Sales Director of anything, do I?"

"No, you don't now, but—"

"I don't look like anything. And do you know why? The answer's because I'm not anything. I have no money, no home, no wife, nothing."

180

Yet again Mrs. Pargeter asserted quietly, "You are Rod Cotton."

Another slow shake of the head. "There is no Rod Cotton. The Rod Cotton you describe was rich, successful. There's no Rod Cotton to fit that description now."

This, Mrs. Pargeter reckoned, was as near as she was going to get to an admission of identity. "Do you still call yourself Rod?" she asked gently.

There was a snort of laughter. "I don't call myself anything. I am no one, so I have no name. When the police move me on, I have no name. When I go into the hostels, I have no name." He waved his plastered arm. "When I fall and end up in hospital, I have no name."

The bottle was once again at his lips, and this time the contents were drained completely. A little trickled down the side of his chin and a panicked hand moved up to save this last dreg. He reached his hands out towards Mrs. Pargeter. "The other bottle."

"No. Not until you've told me what I want to know."

He slumped back, disgruntled, against the bench.

"Look, you are Rod Cotton, aren't you?"

"Give me the bottle and I'll be Marlene Dietrich, if you like," he replied with a cracked laugh.

"I want to know two things, Rod . . ."

"Oh yes."

"The first is—what's happened to you in the last six months?"

"What's happened to who?" he asked deviously.

"What's happened to Rod Cotton?"

"Ah, *him*." He spoke as if referring to some mythical figure from another civilisation. "What's happened to *him*?" He paused, trying to reassemble his scrambled thoughts. Then he launched into a rambling explanation.

"What happened to him was that he couldn't cope with failure. I think. He never failed . . . or so I heard. He passed exams, he got jobs, he was offered other jobs, he made money . . . He didn't fail . . ."

The rambling petered out. Mrs. Pargeter filled the silence. "So, when he lost his job, he didn't know how to set about looking for another one . . . ?"

"He knew how . . ." The tramp halted. "He knew how, but he couldn't . . ."

"You mean mentally he couldn't? He couldn't adjust his mind to the idea?"

The wild head nodded slowly. "He waited. He had a little money, the redundancy money . . . He thought something would happen. He couldn't go out and tell people. He couldn't admit . . ."

"He couldn't admit that he'd failed?" She got no reaction to that. "Which was why he invented the new job, the job up North?"

There was no direct reaction to this question, either, but the tramp suddenly started out on another monologue, as if broaching a new subject.

"He stayed around at home for a while, waiting for it all to be all right, waiting for the phone to ring with the new offer, new job . . . He passed the time with drink, with drugs . . . the phone didn't ring. He went away, just to get away. Went to hotels, nice hotels . . . flash the Gold Card, pay for the hotels . . . Then the hotels don't take the Gold Card. Redundancy money running out. Smaller hotels . . . nastier hotels . . . Bed and breakfast . . . But," he said suddenly, as if quoting something he found very funny, "you don't need bed, you don't need breakfast. To find yourself, you have to get away from material things . . ."

"Is that what Theresa said?" asked Mrs. Pargeter gently.

He didn't confirm this, but let out a grunt of laughter. "Somebody said it, certainly. What they didn't say, though, was that to *lose* yourself, you have to get rid of material things, too. Rod Cotton . . . if that's the name of the person you're talking about? . . . he got rid of material things. Got rid of bed, got rid of breakfast. Don't need a bed." He turned the empty whisky bottle eloquently upside-down. "Don't need much for breakfast."

Again he reached towards her for the second bottle. Mrs. Pargeter shook her head firmly.

He hunched his shoulders and sank back into his greatcoat. "It doesn't take long," he mumbled. "Doesn't take long to get back to a state of. . ." He fumbled for the word. ". . . a state of nature? A state of nothing, a state of not being. It's all just a sort of shell. Money . . . Gold Card . . . job . . . Jacuzzi . . . take it away and there's nothing in the middle . . . Oh yes, you build up a network of money, of greed, but when you slip through the network . . . you go into free fall . . . free fall . . ."

The mental effort of this long speech seemed to have exhausted him. Or maybe it was the half-bottle of scotch. He mumbled incomprehensibly. Then the mumbling triggered a deep, deep cough, which shook his fragile frame.

After the spasm he looked vaguely at Mrs. Pargeter, as if seeing her for the first time. "What do you want?" he asked blankly.

"It's more a matter of what you want," she answered, drawing the second half-bottle of whisky out of her raincoat pocket.

His eyes registered the familiar shape and he reached for it. Mrs. Pargeter put it back out of sight. "I want to talk about Theresa . . ."

The name triggered no reaction at all.

"When did you last see Theresa?"

He shrugged, uncomprehending. The semi-lucid phase had passed; he was now drifting, outside time and reality.

"Do you know how long it is since you left Smithy's Loam?"

"Left where?" The shaggy head shook slowly. "Left . . . ? I don't know . . ."

"Your home. Where you had a wife," Mrs. Pargeter prompted.

"Had a wife . . ." This sparked some recollection for him. "Had a wife, yes. Married." He nodded. "Married a long time ago . . ."

"How long?"

This question was too hard. "Years . . . ?" he hazarded blearily. "Five . . . ten years . . . ?"

It sounded genuine. Mrs. Pargeter could not believe that this human wreck was capable of acting its bewilderment. Nor, come to that, could she believe that it had been capable of executing the carefully planned murder of Theresa Cotton.

But she had to check, had to get something more positive. "Two and a half weeks ago, the Monday of the week before last," she began firmly, "where were you?"

He looked at her as if she had suddenly started speaking in a foreign language. "Huh?"

"Did you go to Smithy's Loam two and a half weeks ago?"

He turned his head in slow confusion. "I don't know. I was here . . . I think. I'm always here. Always round here . . . always round about . . . When I'm not in prison . . . Or hospital . . ." He tapped his grubby plaster. "Hospital . . ."

"When did you break your arm?" Mrs. pargeter asked.

"Broke it. Broken . . . my arm. Then . . . I don't know . . . Fell down . . ." His eyes focused for a split-second. "Where's the bottle?"

"In a moment." Mrs. Pargeter signalled to Truffler Mason, who was seated on a bench a few yards away, maintaining his surveillance over the top of a newspaper. He nodded, taking in the instruction. Casually, he reached into his pocket for a Polaroid camera, rose to his feet and ambled past the two on the opposite bench. As he came level, he took a close-up photograph of the tramp beside Mrs. Pargeter. Rod Cotton gave no sign of having noticed what had happened. He seemed to have sunk into a kind of coma.

"When have you got to go back to the hospital?" Mrs. Pargeter asked.

He looked at her blankly.

"For your arm . . . ?"

He did not appear to understand this, either. Mrs. Pargeter tried more questions, but all of them were met by the same vacant incomprehension. His eyelids were heavy. He looked as if he were about to doze off.

Mrs. Pargeter knew she wouldn't get much more out of him. She beckoned Truffler Mason across. "Did you get a decent shot?"

He showed her the picture, and she nodded. "Better go now, I think."

She hesitated for a moment, and then withdrew the second whisky bottle from her pocket. She looked down at the comatose wreck of humanity beside her. "Do you think I should give it to him? I said I would."

Truffler shrugged. "Don't think it'll make much difference. He doesn't look long for this world, anyway."

"No . . ." Still she hesitated.

"It'd give him a happy hour or two," said Truffler.

She nodded and, still uncertain, held the bottle out.

The engrimed hands instantly reached across and snatched it away. The metal top was unscrewed in one movement and a heavy slug of whisky poured through the discoloured lips. Then the bottle was closed and tucked safely into the greatcoat.

Rod Cotton's shadowed eyes looked up at her pitifully. "Have you got any money?"

"If I gave you money, you'd only spend it on more drink."

He shook his head. "Not drink," he said childishly. "Not drink."

"Food . . . ?"

"Not drink," he asserted once again.

Mrs. Pargeter looked for advice to Truffler Mason, but all she got was another shrug. She'd have to make up her own mind.

And she wasn't the sort of women to resist the pathetic appeal in Rod Cotton's eyes. Impulsively, she unclasped her handbag, reached into her purse and pulled out a fifty-pound note. Then she added another and held them out to the sad figure on the bench.

Truffler Mason looked away as the money was secreted in the filthy recesses of the greatcoat. Rod Cotton gave a slight grin, then his eyes closed, his mouth fell slackly open and he snored, his breath steaming in the cold air of Embankment Gardens.

"God," murmured Mrs. Pargeter. "Isn't there anything we can do to help him?"

Truffler Mason shrugged miserably. "Only if he wants to help himself."

"Mm."

"And from what I've seen, I wouldn't say he does want to help himself. I'd say he wants to destroy himself—and as quickly as possible."

"Yes," said Mrs. Pargeter, suddenly overwhelmed by the bleakness of this undoubted truth. "Yes, I'm afraid you're right."

CHAPTER THIRTY

They picked up the car again in Northumberland Avenue. Gary had been given instructions to circle round until they were ready. Mrs. Pargeter and Truffler got into the back of the limousine in silence. The customary cheerfulness was gone from her face, and his looked even more lugubrious than usual.

Mrs. Pargeter gave terse instructions to the chauffeur, who took them on a tour of the London hospitals. At each one, Mrs. Pargeter stayed in the car, while Truffler, the professional investigator, went into the Casualty Department with his Polaroid photograph.

He struck lucky at the third hospital. The sister he encountered had been on duty when Rod Cotton had been brought in with his broken arm. She recognised the face in the photograph instantly.

Yes, it had been a fall. He had been brought in with advanced DTs, and they'd had to dry him out a bit before they could set the arm. As a result, he had spent three days in the hospital, before discharging himself. No, he had given no name, and appeared to have no address.

She was gloomy about his prospects. They had plenty in like that, and most of them would come in more than once. Falls, walking into lamp-posts, stepping in front of cars. The hospital patched them up, tried to counsel them to change their habits, and, with little optimism, sent them out again into the world they hated, to repeat their accidents. Until one day there was a more serious accident and what arrived in Casualty was a body.

She answered all of Truffler's questions as economically as she could, and then went off to deal with that day's catalogue of human disasters.

He got back into the car, and Mrs. Pargeter told the chauffeur to drive her back to Smithy's Loam. They would drop Mr. Mason off at a Tube station on the way.

"Well?" she said, when the limousine was in motion.

Truffler gave her all the details that he had elicited from the sister.

"And when was this?" asked Mrs. Pargeter.

He gave her the dates. She smiled with grim satisfaction. Rod Cotton's accident had happened on a Sunday evening, nineteen days before. Dead drunk, he had fallen down a flight of steps on Hungerford Bridge and broken his arm. He had been admitted to the hospital at half-past ten that night.

And, since he was kept in there for three days, there

was no way that he could have been at Smithy's Loam the day after the accident, murdering his wife.

Just as Mrs. Pargeter was tipping her chauffeur back at Smithy's Loam, Sue Curle's car screeched to a halt opposite, and its owner scrambled out in high fury. She was met at the door by Kirsten and, after a muttered consultation, the two children were hurried out of the house into the back of the car and all four drove off at speed.

Mrs. Pargeter wondered mildly what all that was about, but she had more pressing thoughts on her mind. There was the small matter of the police that required a decision.

Now, Mrs. Pargeter did not believe in being deliberately obstructive to the police, except of course when it was absolutely necessary to do so. And in this instance, she couldn't really pretend that it was absolutely necessary. Could she?

With a twinge of regret, she admitted to herself that no, she really couldn't.

So, once again, she rang the police informer from the late Mr. Pargeter's address book and gave him the information to pass on.

As a result of his call, by that evening, the official investigators of Theresa Cotton's murder knew where to find the dead woman's husband.

They did not, however, know of his alibi for the time of his wife's murder. Mrs. Pargeter didn't want to make it too easy for them. If they didn't have to work some of the details out for themselves, it took the fun away, didn't it?

Once again, Mrs. Pargeter felt that she was playing fair by the police. She did not want to solve the case by taking unfair advantage of them, so each time she found an important new gobbet of information, she behaved very correctly, and passed it on.

Unfortunately, this was not a reciprocal arrangement.

The police could not be blamed for that state of affairs. Apart from anything else, even if they had wished to repay information with information, they were unaware of the identity of their benefactor, so would not know where to direct it.

And, being the realistic woman she was, Mrs. Pargeter recognised that, even if they knew of her interest in the case, the police might be disinclined to be as generous as she in keeping her abreast of developments in their investigation.

The result of this, however, was that it was some days before Mrs. Pargeter heard of the circumstances in which the police did find Rod Cotton.

As intended, the anonymous tip-off led them to the Embankment, but their quarry was not there when they arrived, and rigorous enquiries amongst his fellow-dossers produced no clue to his whereabouts.

It was three days later, when a body was washed up at Woolwich, that the police identified it as that of Rod Cotton.

And it was not until Tuesday, four days after her encounter with the dead man, that Mrs. Pargeter read this news in her daily paper.

In the report of the discovery, reference was made to Theresa's murder. In the inimitably British way that newspapers have of tiptoeing around the Law, the report im-

plied, without of course saying as much, that the two
deaths were not unconnected.

And also implied, though with what basis of truth could
not be assessed, that the police might be looking no further
for the murderer of Theresa Cotton.

CHAPTER THIRTY-ONE

In all her deliberations about the case, Mrs. Pargeter kept coming back to the same question. How much could the murderer have predicted?

The murderer could not have predicted, for example, that Theresa's body would have been found as soon as it was. On the other hand, he or she could have predicted that it would have been found at some point. So that risk must have been taken into account.

The murderer could also have predicted that, once the murder was discovered, the first person the police were likely to look for was Rod Cotton. Now, if Rod, as the accepted wisdom of Smithy's Loam had it, was working in the North, the police would have had no difficulty at all in tracking him down. And, once they had tracked him down, they would question him about his movements at the time of his wife's murder. That time was in fact a very specific and relatively short period. Theresa Cotton had been seen, alive and well, at about seven-thirty on the Monday evening, by Sid Runcorn the car dealer. And she had been safely strangled and stowed away in her freezer by nine o'clock the following morning when Littlehaven's removal men arrived.

So, if the conjectural Rod Cotton who worked in the North of England had an alibi for that crucial thirteen-and-a-half-hour period—and there was a very good chance that he would have—then his usefulness to the murderer as a decoy quickly evaporated.

The real Rod Cotton, on the other hand, the drunken, unfocused, washed-up Rod Cotton, who wandered through London without a name or a home, was a much better proposition. Mrs. Pargeter had been very fortunate in discovering his alibi for the time of the murder; he was certainly in no state to provide it himself. Anyway, he had to be found first, and it had taken all of the exceptional skills of Truffler Mason to achieve that.

So the murderer might well have felt pretty safe with the real Rod Cotton as a suspect. Rod was one of the lost people of England, one who had lost his identity completely, had simply slipped off the demographic map of the country's population.

There was a comforting kind of logic to it. The first suspect is the victim's spouse, because the first suspect always *is* the victim's spouse. But then the victim's spouse can't be found, suggesting that he has done a bunk and reinforcing the existing suspicions against him.

Yes, it made sense.

Assuming of course that the murderer knew about what had really happened to Rod Cotton.

It became a priority for Mrs. Pargeter to find out how many of the residents of Smithy's Loam had been taken in by the story of his promotion and transfer to the North of England.

And the resident who warranted most urgent investigation was the one who, Mrs. Pargeter suspected, had been rather closer to Rod Cotton than the others.

"Well, obviously," said Vivvi Sprake, "the news of the last few weeks has been pretty devastating. I mean, first Theresa, and then Rod . . . it's ghastly."

Mrs. Pargeter nodded sympathetically. She had had no problem at all in getting Vivvi on to the desired subject. Advice on gardeners had been quickly dispensed, and Vivvi herself had brought up the murder. She had been longing to have a really good natter about it, and she thought Mrs. Pargeter might be a more enthusiastic participant in gossip than the other, more stand-offish, residents of Smithy's Loam. She felt drawn to the older woman; though Mrs. Pargeter's background was London, her relaxed conversational approach struck chords from Vivvi's northern upbringing.

"I mean, it's dreadful . . . you know, to think that people you've known . . . could do that to each other."

"Dreadful. Impossible to see inside another couple's marriage," Mrs. Pargeter commented, masking her interest in the platitude, and noting that Vivvi, at least apparently, accepted the prevalent view that Rod had killed his wife.

"Yes. Yes," Vivvi agreed, and couldn't help adding mysteriously, "Mind you, I don't think everything was as sunny as it seemed with the Cottons' marriage . . ."

"Oh?" said Mrs. Pargeter, without too much emphasis. She didn't think that Vivvi was going to be too difficult a subject to interrogate; indeed, she thought the problem might later be to stem the flow of confidences.

"Yes . . . Well, I'm only telling you this in confidence, Mrs. Pargeter . . ."

"Of course, of course . . ."

"But Rod Cotton once made a pass at me."

"Really?" said Mrs. Pargeter, as if dumbfounded.

"Oh yes," Vivvi Sprake asserted with a harsh woman-of-the-world laugh that didn't quite come off.

"When was this?"

"Rod was around for a while between finishing the job down here and moving up to the new job in York . . ."

Vivvi was the first of the Smithy's Loam crowd to mention "York" as opposed to just "the North." That, like the fact that she had had Rod's office phone number, confirmed the idea of a special relationship between the two.

"Anyway, I went across one morning round that time —to give something to Theresa, actually—but she wasn't there and Rod invited me in . . ."

"And made a pass at you?"

"Well, in a way, yes. The fact is, I was going through a rather unhappy time myself . . ."

Mrs. Pargeter tried another little "Oh?" They seemed to be working very well, her little "Oh?"s.

This one proved no exception. Vivvi was desperate to pour it all out. "The fact is, you see, that Nigel . . . my husband, has been married before. I'm his second wife."

"Really?"

"Yes. I was his secretary and, er, we fell in love and, er, well, that was it. He left his wife for me and, you

know, we had the children quite soon, and here we are."
As Vivvi got deeper into confidences, her accent became
increasingly northern. "Very happy we are. All works very
well."

"Oh, good."

"However . . ." Vivvi paused, almost as if she was considering not continuing. But there was no real chance of
that; she was enjoying the drama of her narrative far too
much. "Well, there was a patch about six months ago
when . . . I suppose you'd have to say . . . things weren't
perfect between us for a while . . ."

"Oh?"

"Just briefly. Nigel was . . . the fact is . . . Look, I am
telling you this in complete confidence . . ."

"Of course. I have taught myself to be very discreet,
you know, Vivvi." Only the late Mr. Pargeter knew how
thoroughly true that remark was.

Vivvi Sprake needed no further reassurance. "Well, the
fact is, I discovered that Nigel, my husband, was having
a little fling with his current secretary . . ."

"Oh. History repeating itself."

"No," Vivvi contradicted sharply. "Well, not at all in
the same way. I mean, this girl was some dreadful little
tart who was just infatuated with him—he is a very attractive man—and, you know, she led him on . . . I mean,
it was nothing like our affair . . ."

"Of course not," said Mrs. Pargeter, translating Vivvi's
words into the fact that the new secretary, unlike her pred-
ecessor, hadn't got pregnant.

"Anyway, everything's absolutely fine now. I mean, Nigel's deeply sorry it happened, and of course nothing like
that'll ever happen again."

Like hell, thought Mrs. Pargeter.

". . . but the fact remains that six months ago I was feeling pretty bad about it, pretty vulnerable . . ."

"I'm sure you were. So probably you didn't respond to Rod quite as you would have done under normal circumstances . . . ?"

Vivvi seemed very grateful to Mrs. Pargeter for spelling this out.

"Exactly. That was it. Under normal circumstances I would have just slapped his hand or . . . but, well, as I say I was feeling vulnerable . . ."

"And fairly angry, too, I should think."

"Oh yes, extremely angry. So . . ."

"I don't think anyone could have blamed you," said Mrs. Pargeter comfortingly.

"No. Well, I certainly had been provoked."

"I'll say. Tit-for-tat's pretty reasonable in my book."

"Yes. Oh, you're very understanding, Mrs. Pargeter. It really is a pleasure for me to unburden myself to someone. I've been bottling it all up and, you know, well, particularly now, after what's happened . . ."

"Yes."

"And, I mean, Rod was a very attractive man."

"I'm sure he was." But all Mrs. Pargeter could see in her mind's eye was the hunched, decrepit figure on the bench in Embankment Gardens.

"And, you know, he got me very relaxed and . . ."

"What, he gave you a drink?"

"Yes." Vivvi Sprake giggled mischievously. "Not just a drink . . ."

"Oh?"

Once again the monosyllable worked a treat. "Recreational drugs, Mrs. Pargeter."

"Ah."

"Cocaine."

"Really?"

"Well, Rod was in a very stressful job, you know."

"Yes." Even more stressful when he lost it.

"So, anyway," Vivvi went on, "one thing led to another . . ."

"Or *the* other . . . ?" Mrs. Pargeter offered cheekily.

Vivvi giggled. "Yes. Exactly."

"Just the once, was it?"

"Well . . ." She blushed. "Once or twice. Four times, actually."

"Oh. And did your husband ever find out?"

"No. Oh, good heavens, no. No, Nigel'd kill me if he ever found out. He's got a terrible temper." The younger woman looked suddenly frightened. "Mrs. Pargeter, you must promise me you'll never breathe a word about this. I shouldn't have told you."

"Don't worry. Nothing goes beyond these four walls," Mrs. Pargeter reassured her. Then suddenly she asked, "What about Theresa?"

"Theresa?"

"Did she know about it?"

Vivvi coloured. "No. Of course not." But for the first time that morning, she seemed anxious to move the conversation on, rather than to linger lovingly on its details. Mrs. Pargeter had a shrewd suspicion she knew what had been said when Theresa Cotton visited "Haymakers" on the night she died.

"But the affair didn't continue . . . ?"

"No. Well, Rod started his new job and, you know, I said it ought to end . . ."

"Of course," said Mrs. Pargeter, reading between the

lines and understanding that it was Rod who had said it ought to end.

Vivvi seemed suddenly struck by remorse. "And now he's dead," she said, wallowing in the emotion of the thought.

"Yes."

"But, Mrs. Pargeter," she went on with sudden alarm, "you won't breathe a word about this to anyone, will you?"

"No, of course not."

"I shouldn't have told you."

"Don't worry. As I said, none of it will go any further than these four walls. Promise."

Vivvi looked relieved. "Oh thank you, Mrs. Pargeter."

"No problem. One thing . . . ?" she added diffidently.

"Yes?"

"While this affair was going on, did you meet in the Cottons' house?"

"Good heavens, no." Vivvi sounded appalled by the idea. "What, have an affair in Smithy's Loam?" She spoke reverentially, as if referring to holy ground. "Everyone'd know immediately. No, we went to a motel."

"What, even the first time?"

"Yes. I mean, he made the pass in the house, that's when he made the suggestion, but then we agreed to meet for lunch later in the week . . ."

"At the motel?"

"Yes." Vivvi blushed at the recollection. "God, I felt terrible that week."

"Hm, yes, well, I suppose you would." Mrs. Pargeter thought for a moment. "And, Vivvi, after Rod started his new job, did you ever try to contact him?"

"In York?"

"Mm."

"Well, I did think about it, yes, but, I don't know, I decided it probably wasn't a good idea. You know, when something's finished . . ."

"Yes . . ."

"I mean, once *I'd* decided it was finished . . ."

"Yes, of course," said Mrs. Pargeter cosily. "Very sensible."

She felt convinced that Vivvi Sprake had believed completely in Rod Cotton's new job in York. So that answered the question which had prompted Mrs. Pargeter to set up the interview.

On the other hand, their conversation had also raised some new questions.

Very interesting questions, to Mrs. Pargeter's way of thinking.

CHAPTER THIRTY-TWO

That evening Mrs. Pargeter lay long in a hot bath, still thinking about the murder in Smithy's Loam. Slowly, she once again went through all the elements of the case, testing them out, linking facts and pulling them tight, checking out whether there were any holes in her logic, any details she was missing out.

But nothing new came to her, no blinding insight into the identity of Theresa Cotton's killer. Everything else in the case made sense; the shape, the outline was clear; but there remained a great hole at the centre. One unanswered question: who had actually done it?

Mrs. Pargeter had narrowed down the list of suspects. She was now convinced that Theresa Cotton had been killed by one of the women in Smithy's Loam. And that the reason for the murder was something that had been said during Theresa's conscience-clearing circuit of the other houses in the close early on the evening she died.

To all of the women she had revealed that she knew secrets about them. But to one the secret was so important that she was prepared to kill to keep it quiet.

Mrs. Pargeter was slowly building up a list of what those secrets might be, but as yet her list was incomplete.

When she got out of the bath and wrapped herself in a sheet-size bath towel, Mrs. Pargeter felt cold. There was a draught coming from behind the curtain. Must have left the fanlight open.

She reached up to release the prop that held the window ajar, but it wouldn't budge. She climbed up on a bathroom chair and, with the curtain bunching round her like a cloak, tried to shift the jammed lock.

It gave after a moment's effort and she closed the window. She was just about to step down from the chair when she saw something that froze her where she was.

The bathroom was on the side of the house, facing the Temples'. Up to fanlight level, the window glass was discreetly frosted, but above that it was plain. And through this plain glass Mrs. Pargeter could see into Carole and Gregory Temple's bedroom.

The curtains were only half-drawn, which was strange.

But not as strange as what Mrs. Pargeter could see through them.

She saw a backview which must be Carole, though somehow it didn't look like Carole. Anyway, surely she had seen Carole's car leaving just before running her bath . . . ?

And why would Carole be dressing up so elaborately and preening herself in front of the mirror? She was wearing a low-backed red satin cocktail dress, stockings and silver high-heeled shoes. The ensemble didn't conform with her customary rather dour style of dress.

Still, perhaps she was going out to some smart function in the near future and was just testing the effect.

But the way she was preening and parading in front of the mirror also seemed at odds with what Mrs. Pargeter knew of her neighbour's character. There was something strange in her movements, too. Could Carole Temple possibly be drunk?

Suddenly the figure in front of the mirror turned to check the straightness of her stocking seams in the mirror.

It wasn't the unaccustomed heaviness of the make-up that took Mrs. Pargeter by surprise—it was the moustache.

The oddness of the figure was suddenly explained. It wasn't Carole Temple who was preening herself in the red cocktail dress—it was her husband, Gregory.

Hmm, thought Mrs. Pargeter, now that *is* interesting.

Suppose Theresa Cotton had witnessed a similar parade on a previous evening when Carole Temple had been out . . .

And suppose she had told Carole Temple what she had seen . . .

Might not that be the sort of secret that should be kept from spreading amongst the other residents of Smithy's Loam?

CHAPTER THIRTY-THREE

"God, that bloody girl!" said Sue Curle, relaxing as she made her way down the second of Mrs. Pargeter's generous gin and tonics. "She's just so disorganised. I mean suddenly there's this flap last week because she's forgotten about her visa and it's about to run out, and so I get this panic call at the office, because she's got to go up to the Norwegian Embassy and she can't leave the kids and . . ." She growled. "God, it is nearly impossible to hold down a job and run a home at the same time."

"I thought an *au pair* was supposed to make it possible."

"Huh!" was all that idea was thought to deserve.

"But at least everything's all right at work, isn't it . . . ?" asked Mrs. Pargeter cautiously.

"I suppose so . . . when I'm there. When I don't keep getting called back home on idiotic errands."

"Yes. Actually, Sue, I don't even know what it is you do . . . ?"

"Market research company."

"Local, obviously."

"Yes, in Dorking. Started up by a bloke I used to work with before I got nailed down by marriage and children. He went on his own about five years back and it all seems to be going well. Get market research right and you can't fail."

"A lot of companies do fail, though, don't they?"

"Ah, yes, but that's because they *don't* get it right. Geoff—that's my boss—is a very shrewd operator. Knows what he's doing. If a firm's doing badly, he persuades them that they need market research to find out *why* they're doing badly. If they're doing well, he persuades them they need it to do even better."

"Sounds good. And of course it must be nice for you working with people you know."

"Oh, I don't know him that well," said Sue dismissively.

"No, but at least if you're with congenial people . . ."

"Huh. I don't think Geoff could ever be described as congenial," said Sue with some vigour. "He's an absolute pig to work for. Typical male. Good at the job, but very exhausting to be with. No, I'm just very relieved to get away from the office as soon as possible every night."

"But the hours do seem to be long," suggested Mrs. Pargeter. "I mean, I quite often see your car coming back round nine, half-past."

"Yes, well, we do get very busy. When you're a relatively new set-up, you can't afford to turn any work down. There aren't many of us in the company, anyway. And I think perhaps Geoff has to work a bit harder than the opposition."

"Why's that?"

"Well, he's coloured. Born in Jamaica. It's a terrible thing to say, but I'm afraid there still is a bit of prejudice, even in a place like this."

"Oh, really?" said Mrs. Pargeter, keeping to herself the thoughts which had suddenly been set buzzing about her head. Time to change the subject. "Any nearer getting your divorce through, are you?"

This got another of Sue's bitter little "Huh"s. "No, that bastard is dragging everything out for as long as possible. Never marry a lawyer, Mrs. Pargeter."

"I don't think I'm really likely to at my age." It wasn't just age that was a bar, now she came to think of it. Certain basic differences of attitude on certain issues might lead to marital discord, too.

"No. Well, don't," said Sue grimly. "That would be my advice to anyone of any age. Because the Law is just a system of institutionalised delay and if you've got a lawyer against you in a divorce, he can keep on finding loopholes and legal quirks and quibbles until you're almost driven mad. And if he happens to be the person you're trying to divorce . . . huh, well, it's even worse."

"It must be very frustrating for you."

"You can say that again. And nothing's sacred to a bloody lawyer. He's quite happy for all the secrets of our marriage to be dragged through the courts."

"Doesn't your husband actually want to get divorced?"

"He says he doesn't. Treated me like a dog all the time we were together and then, when I kick him out, suddenly he becomes all maudlin and pathetic and keeps on about

207

how he misses the kids and . . . huh, snivelling little wimp."

"So is he fighting you for custody of the kids?"

"He's trying to. Mind you, he won't succeed. I'll see to that. There is no way I'm going to allow that bum to have more to do with *my* children than is absolutely necessary.'" Sue Curle made this pronouncement with an intensity that was almost frightening.

Time to shift the subject again. "Well, lots of luck, Sue. I'm sure it'll work out for you."

"Bloody well hope so." She suddenly remembered something. "Ooh, Mrs. Pargeter. Next Monday."

"What about it?"

"Put it in your diary. I'm going to have this meeting about the Indian restaurant."

"What, your Women's Action Group thing?"

"That's it. Six o'clock my place. Before the husbands get home. You will come, won't you?"

"Well, yes, I'll come. Though I must confess I'm not sure which side I'm on . . ."

"Not sure?" Sue Curle stared at her in amazement. "There's only one side to be on. We don't want an Indian restaurant on the corner of Smithy's Loam, do we?"

And the contempt she put into the word "Indian" confirmed her own earlier observation that there really still *was* a bit of prejudice about.

"Well, Sue, I'll certainly be there. Look forward to it." Another graceful change of subject was called for. "Everything settling down a bit now in Smithy's Loam, isn't it?" said Mrs. Pargeter pacifically.

"What do you mean?"

"Well, after the murder. I mean, no more policemen popping out asking questions at every turn . . ."

"No."

"I suppose they are pretty certain that Rod killed her."

"Seems most likely, doesn't it?"

"Hmm. Goodness, though, they did go on, didn't they? I gather they were asking everyone when they last saw Theresa . . ."

"Well, they have to. That's their job, isn't it?"

"Oh, yes, yes. No, I was quite glad I wasn't living here at the time. After I heard all the questions everyone else had to answer. Enough to make you feel guilty even if you've never done anything wrong in your life."

Sue Curle didn't join in the chuckle that accompanied this.

"Yes, it seems," Mrs. Pargeter went on, "that Theresa Cotton went round saying goodbye to everyone in the close . . ."

"Yes," Sue Curle agreed shortly.

"Oh, I'm sorry." Mrs. Pargeter shook her head at her own stupidity. "We've had this conversation, haven't we?"

"I believe we did talk about it, yes."

" 'Cause you said that you'd had to come home early from the office because Kirsten was up in London . . ."

"That's right."

"And Theresa came to see you . . ."

"Yes."

"Just to say goodbye . . . ?"

"That's right," said Sue Curle firmly. "Just to say goodbye."

There was such a thing, Mrs. Pargeter reflected after her guest had left, as protesting too much. She might have suspected some of that was going on from the way Sue badmouthed her boss, even if she hadn't seen them together looking so intimate in that pub but as it was . . .

So Sue was trying to throw people off the scent about her relationship with Geoff. Might not that suggest that her "working late at the office" was as much of a euphemism as the expression traditionally is . . . ?

And might not knowledge of her affair be just the sort of ammunition her lawyer husband would seize on in his battle to gain custody of their children . . . ? Even to the extent of playing on the undoubted colour prejudice there was around . . . ?

Suppose Theresa Cotton had known about the affair and "cleared her mind of grudges and resentments" by telling Sue that she knew . . .

And suppose Sue had translated Theresa's words into a threat to tell all to her husband . . .

Given the ferocity with which she was determined to hang on to her children, it looked as if Sue Curle was another Smithy's Loam resident with a possible motive for murder.

CHAPTER THIRTY-FOUR

Of course, there was someone else in Smithy's Loam who might be capable of a totally irrational act like murder. Jane Watson gave every appearance of being completely mad, and, in her paranoid delusions, the permanent removal of someone who represented a threat to her might seem completely logical.

But Mrs. Pargeter didn't like that conclusion. For a start, she had a strong prejudice against murders committed by people who were mad. She had always disliked them in crime fiction and didn't care for them much in real life. Madness was so vague, so woolly. Any motivation and logic could be ascribed to someone who was mad. At the end of a crime book in which a madman dunnit, Mrs. Pargeter always felt cheated and annoyed.

Apart from anything else, the murder of Theresa Cotton did not look like the work of someone unhinged. It had not been an irrational act; rather the reverse, it had been a supremely rational act. Putting on one side for a moment the theory that the taking of human life is an act of madness under any circumstances, the strangling had been well thought out and executed.

No, it was simplistic to say: Jane Watson appears to be mad, therefore Jane Watson must have killed Theresa Cotton.

Anyway, even madness has its logic. There are reasons behind most irrational behaviour, even though those reasons often only make sense to the perpetrator of that behaviour. What Jane Watson had said to Mrs. Pargeter had contained an internal logic for her, if not for anyone else. And the more Mrs. Pargeter thought about their encounter inside "Hibiscus," the more she seemed to see a logic running through Jane Watson's behaviour. Jane had not randomly identified Mrs. Pargeter as an enemy; something in her visitor's actions or behaviour had triggered that response.

Mrs. Pargeter concentrated hard, and thought through everything that had happened that morning, and everything that had happened on every other occasion when her path had crossed with that of Jane Watson.

It took about ten minutes of thinking back, recreating the scenes, remembering the minutiae, and then suddenly all became clear.

The important encounter had been the one a few weeks before when Mrs. Pargeter had gone across to see Fiona Burchfield-Brown and check on the identity of Theresa Cotton's first bearded visitor. As she came out of "High

212

Bushes" she had almost bumped into Jane Watson. And Jane Watson had looked at her and run away as if scared out of her wits.

What Mrs. Pargeter had forgotten until that moment was what she had been carrying on that occasion. Held against her chest had been the booklets of the Church of Utter Simplicity.

She began to see daylight. If one identified the "them" of Jane Watson's paranoid ramblings with the members of the Church, a kind of logic emerged.

The police informer agreed that it was not his usual line of work. But, still, he worked a lot on the telephone and yes, of course he'd do it. Anything that the widow of the late Mr. Pargeter required, whatever it was, no problem, he'd be happy to oblige.

"Say you're a television researcher," said Mrs. Pargeter.

"OK."

"And say you're researching a programme into dubious religious sects. And say that your aim is to expose some of the things they do . . . like brainwashing, or putting obstacles in the way of people who want to leave."

"Right you are."

"Do assure her that your aim is to have these abuses put right. And assure her that anything she says will be treated in absolute confidence, that nobody will ever know she told you . . ."

"OK."

"Say I gave you her name . . ."

"You, Mrs. Pargeter?"

"That's right. Say that I am determined to have the practices of this kind of place stopped at all costs . . ."

"Anything else?"

"That'll do for the time being. Ring me back and tell me how she takes it."

"OK."

He rang half an hour later. "Sorry I couldn't get back to you before. She talked."

"Had a lot to say?"

"You could put it like that, Mrs. Pargeter, yes. Very difficult to stop her once she got started. Pretty highly strung lady, I'd say."

Yes, highly strung, thought Mrs. Pargeter, but not mad.

"Anyway, I got it all. That Church does sound a pretty dodgy set-up, I must say."

"They wouldn't let her leave?"

"That seemed to be her main problem, yes. Apparently even now, five years after she got out, she still lives in fear that they're sending off people to fetch her back in."

Yes, it all fitted. Mrs. Pargeter thanked her unseen assistant profusely, and once again received assurances that, after all the late Mrs. Pargeter had done for him, nothing was too much trouble.

"No, I can fully understand," said Mrs. Pargeter, trying to stem Jane Watson's flow.

"I'm sorry, but once I finally did get out of that place, I cracked up completely. You know, a really major breakdown. Lasted eighteen months or so. But I had help and drugs and things and gradually I began to come out of it. And then I met Roger and we got married and moved here, and I really thought things'd be all right. I mean, I was still in a strange state . . . you know, afraid of people, terrified of making contact. I'd just lost all my confidence about dealing with things. But Roger's wonderfully supportive, I'm so lucky. And I really thought I was getting better."

"Until Theresa mentioned that she was going to join the Church, too."

Jane Watson became suddenly devious. "I didn't say she said that."

"No, but—"

"No, actually, the thing that sparked it all off again was seeing someone from . . . someone from . . ." She couldn't bring herself to say the words. ". . . someone from that place, here, in Smithy's Loam."

"Brother Brian?"

Jane Watson nodded. "I saw him going up Theresa's front path. I thought he was coming for me and had gone to the wrong house. I'm afraid I just went. Instantly I was right back like at the beginning of the breakdown. I hid. I locked myself in the lavatory."

"But Brother Brian didn't come to your door, did he?"

"No, but I was convinced they were on to me. I was convinced that they'd tracked me down. And I thought they'd take me away from my house and from Roger and—"

"They haven't got the power to do that, Jane."

"Oh, they have. They're very powerful, Mrs. Pargeter, very persuasive."

"Yes, but you've got free of them, you really have. You've broken away and made your own life, outside the Church of Utter Simplicity."

"I know," said Jane. "I know I have." She didn't sound very convinced by her assertion. "But when I see them again, I just feel utterly powerless."

"You'll be all right," Mrs. Pargeter soothed. "Even if they did know where you are, they'd have given you up as a bad job by now. Anyway, they got all your money when you joined, didn't they?"

The woman nodded.

"That's all they're really interested in."

"Yes, but now I'm well-off again. I mean, Roger's got a good job and . . ."

"Jane, that is your husband's money. He's not going to give it to some loony sect, is he?"

"No, no, I suppose not. I'm sorry, I do just panic when I see anything to do with them. I'm not rational."

"Which is why you rushed away when you saw me carrying their leaflets?"

"Exactly. I thought you were another one. I just get so confused, I'm not really responsible for what I do."

"Listen . . ." Mrs. Pargeter took the woman's trembling hand. "It's all right. You're quite safe here. There's no one out to get you."

"No?"

"No."

"Oh, I know you're right. I still just panic when I meet people."

"Well, you needn't. Come on, you must get to know your neighbours. They don't mean you any harm. They can even help you."

Jane didn't look convinced by this assertion. Mrs. Pargeter wondered how much she was convinced by it herself. One at least of the other Smithy's Loam residents had proved unhelpful to the point of murdering someone.

Unless, of course, it had been Jane herself.

"Tell me," Mrs. Pargeter began in a tranquillising tone, "what happened that day Theresa left?"

"Mm?" Jane looked at her blankly, as if she had just dragged back from another plane of being.

"The day you saw Brother Brian . . . ?"

"I don't know. As I say, I just panicked. I took a lot of these pills the doctor had given me."

"Tranquillisers?"

"That kind of thing, yes. They make me all woozy. I don't really know what I'm doing when I have a lot of them. Just walk around in a dream."

"Hm. And did Theresa come and see you?"

"When?"

"That evening. The evening after you'd seen Brother Brian. She went round and said goodbye to everyone else in the close."

"Oh."

"Did she come and see you?"

"Yes. I can't remember. Maybe she did. I think so."

"Came just to say goodbye."

"That's right," said Jane Watson, nodding her head slowly in confirmation. "Just to say goodbye."

No, Jane Watson couldn't be ruled out, either. True, the heavily tranquillised state she was in on the night of the murder did not fit in well with the meticulousness of the crime.

But then there was no guarantee that she was telling the truth about what had happened.

And, given Jane Watson's terror of being taken back there, Theresa Cotton might only have needed to mention the Church of Utter Simplicity to sign her own death warrant.

CHAPTER THIRTY-FIVE

Which really just left Fiona Burchfield-Brown.

Mrs. Pargeter wondered whether there could be anything that Theresa Cotton had challenged Fiona Burchfield-Brown with when she visited her on the night before her death. Fiona seemed so aristocratically bumbling, so earnestly incompetent, so transparent, that it was hard to imagine her as the possessor of a guilty secret. But Mrs. Pargeter was far too canny an old bird to be deceived by appearances.

She settled down that evening over a large vodka Campari to think about what might worry Fiona Burchfield-Brown.

It didn't take long for her to decide to ring Truffler Mason. He had after all investigated the residents of Smithy's Loam in his search for Rod. Was it possible that his Welsh "market researcher" had come up with something that might be relevant?

His voice sounded as mournful as ever, but it contained no trace of resentment. He was still quite happy to give Mrs. Pargeter any assistance she might require.

"I'll ask and get back to you," he said. Then, with a note of concern in his voice, he continued. "Does this mean, Mrs. Pargeter, that you're still on the case . . . ?"

"Well . . ."

"I thought the husband-kills-wife scenario was a bit obvious myself."

"I think it's just worth my asking around a bit," Mrs. Pargeter conceded cautiously. "You know, see if I get any leads."

"Hmm. All right. But you be careful."

"What do you mean, Truffler? I'm not in any danger."

"Don't you believe it. You're up against someone completely ruthless."

"Yes, but I'll keep a low profile and—"

"Look, the murderer has already killed two people to keep whatever secret it is quiet."

"Two?"

"Well, I'd have said quite possibly two, yes, Mrs. Pargeter. Do you really think Rod Cotton fell in the Thames by mistake?"

"I had assumed that, yes. Or it might have been suicide. I mean, he was in such a hopeless state, he had no idea what he was doing. He'd already fallen and had one accident. He could hardly stand up straight."

"Make him all the easier to push in, wouldn't it?"

"I hadn't thought of that."

"Look, Mrs. Pargeter, you've established that the murderer knew about what had happened to Rod Cotton . . ."

"I think so, yes."

"Must be right. Only someone who knew the state he was in would have dared to dispose of the body that way. The murderer was counting on the fact that either the police wouldn't be able to find Rod Cotton or that, if they did, they wouldn't be able to get any sense out of him . . ."

"Yes, I suppose you're right."

"So if Rod had made contact with the murderer recently, the murderer might have reckoned he knew too much for safety."

"But why would Rod make contact?"

"I don't know. Maybe because of something you said when you talked to him . . ."

"Oh, good heavens, I never thought of that."

"I may be wrong. All I'm saying, Mrs. Pargeter, is that you're up against someone who won't hesitate to use violence again. So, if you are planning any heroics—"

"I don't think heroics are my style at all," said Mrs. Pargeter coyly.

"From what I've seen of you, I think they just might be. Anyway if you are planning any kind of confrontation, make sure that I'm around."

"Very well." She spoke contritely, like an obedient little girl. It was rather comforting, though, the thought that she had a protector on hand when she needed one. Comfortingly familiar—it was, after all, a feeling she got used to while the late Mr. Pargeter had been alive.

Truffler rang back within the hour.

"Only found out one thing about the Burchfield-Brown

woman," he announced, like an undertaker discreetly offering his price-list.

"Yes?"

"Well, she's not the genuine article."

"What do you mean?"

"I mean, the accent, all that . . . the education—it's phoney."

"She wasn't at Roedean or finishing schools or anything like that?"

"No. She left a comprehensive in Essex at sixteen and worked in the checkout in Tesco's."

"What? Well, how on earth did she transform herself into this Sloane Ranger figure that she is now?"

"Don't know all the details. She had elocution lessons, certainly, started grooming herself, met a few of the right sort of people, I suppose . . ."

"Married one of the right sort of people?"

"Maybe."

"He must know, though, mustn't he? Alexander, her husband. I mean, she could fool neighbours and people when she moved into a new area, but she couldn't keep that kind of secret from someone she was living with, could she?"

"No, I doubt if she could. But then it seems that he's no more the genuine article than she is."

"What, so all his family silver and Range Rover and upper-crust manners and Hooray Henry accent are just made up?"

"That's the way it seems, Mrs. Pargeter, yes."

She was thoughtful. "It does make sense of certain things, actually. Fiona's constant fear of letting her husband down, for a start. And I suppose actually it's an easy enough front to maintain somewhere like this. You move to a new area, you present yourself as you choose, and people accept you at face value. No problem. Particularly in Smithy's Loam, where nobody's that interested in anyone else, anyway."

"Well, as I say, Mrs. Pargeter, that's it. They're both acting like they've got a social background that they haven't. Common enough deception, I suppose."

"Yes." It was, however, a deception whose necessity Mrs. Pargeter could never understand. Not once in her life had she ever tried to change herself in any particular. People either took her as she was or they didn't. And as for those who didn't . . . well, she never reckoned it was *her* loss.

"But," Truffler went on dolefully, "I mean, that's a secret, OK. But it's not a secret anyone would kill to keep quiet, is it?"

"I'm not so sure," said Mrs. Pargeter. "You don't know what people are like in Smithy's Loam."

CHAPTER THIRTY-SIX

~~~~~~

Now more than ever Mrs. Pargeter felt convinced that Theresa Cotton had been murdered by one of the women in Smithy's Loam. One of the women who had been visited in Theresa's final mind-clearing circuit on the evening she died.

There were five suspects, each with a guilty secret. And if Theresa had confronted each one with those secrets, as seemed likely, then any of the five might have had a motive for murder.

In her mind, Mrs. Pargeter went round the close once more. Fiona Burchfield-Brown in "High Bushes"; in "Perigord," Sue Curle (and of course Kirsten, but Kirsten had not been in at the time of Theresa's confrontations, so she had to be excluded); Vivvi Sprake in "Haymakers"; Jane Watson in "Hibiscus"; and Carole Temple in "Cromarty."

Fiona Burchfield-Brown had to maintain secrecy about her true origins.

Sue Curle was trying to keep quiet the affair with her boss, the West Indian Geoff, desperate lest her husband should find out and use it as a lever in his fight for custody of their children.

Vivvi Sprake had to keep her husband in ignorance of her little flutter with Rod Cotton.

Jane Watson thought that Theresa represented a threat to take her back to the hated Church of Utter Simplicity.

And Carole Temple had no doubt been confronted with the news of her husband's transvestism. Not that it had probably been news to her; for Carole the terrible part would be that someone else knew about it.

Five women with five secrets. And one secret so important to its owner that it could justify murder.

Mrs. Pargeter thought she had done well. She had worked most of it out on her own, and had had an unrivalled support team to follow up her ideas.

But she still hadn't reached the solution. She still didn't know who had killed Theresa Cotton. It was very frustrating.

Hmm, what was that expression Truffler Mason had used? Heroics, yes, that was it.

Maybe, Mrs. Pargeter thought, with an irrepressible flicker of glee, it is time for a few heroics.

CHAPTER THIRTY-SEVEN

It had been quite an achievement for Sue Curle to persuade Jane Watson to come along to the discussion meeting about the proposed Indian restaurant. When receiving hers, Mrs. Pargeter had asked whether an invitation had also been issued to "Hibiscus," and Sue had said no, there was no point, Jane never came to anything. Mrs. Pargeter had been of the opinion that it was still worth trying and made an exploratory phone call herself to prepare the ground. Her words must have been effective, because Sue Curle's invitation was accepted, and Jane Watson, looking nervous but defiant, appeared at "Perigord" on the dot of six o'clock when the meeting was due to start.

It was held in Sue Curle's front room, whose decor favoured the now slightly dated Laura Ashley cowshed look.

Dark brown paint, stripped pine furniture, curtains with little flowers on them, tiny framed Victorian prints and polished agricultural implements hanging on the walls.

Through the hatch to the kitchen, the sound could be heard of Kirsten giving supper to the two subjects of the custody battle. Sue had put wine bottles and glasses out to welcome her guests, though Carole Temple, for one, thought this introduced an unwarranted element of frivolity into the proceedings. "We are here to have a serious meeting," she said, "not a social occasion." And then, in an undertone, "And I still think it's ridiculous not to have the men along."

The others seemed happy enough to accept a drink, though Jane Watson asked for Perrier (tranquillised up to her eyebrows, Mrs. Pargeter reckoned, couldn't risk mixing it with alcohol).

Mrs. Pargeter had come to "Perigord" a fraction early, so that she could monitor the arrival of the other women of Smithy's Loam. She wanted to take a further, contemplative look at each of them, hoping without much hope that one might give some clue to identify her as Theresa Cotton's murderer.

Mrs. Pargeter hadn't quite worked out yet what form her "heroics" were going to take, but she did feel an inward pressure to force the issue, to bring things to a head that evening. Who could say when she'd have another chance of seeing all the women together?

Though the subject of the murder was by now old news, given the short attention-span of the Smithy's Loam residents, its sensational nature did still justify an occasional airing, so Mrs. Pargeter had no difficulty in raising the topic.

"It's really sad, isn't it," she said ruminatively, "to think of what went on inside the Cottons' marriage . . . you know, the kind of pressures that could build up to murder . . ."

"Yes, it is dreadful," Vivvi Sprake agreed in a detached, automatic way.

Fiona Burchfield-Brown supplied the inevitable platitude. "Still, you can never really see inside another marriage."

"No, well, everyone's private life is secret, isn't it? I mean, I'm sure most marriages contain a few secrets which the participants would rather stayed that way."

Mrs. Pargeter stared directly at Carole Temple as she said this, and was rewarded by the other woman looking sharply away and announcing, "I think we really should get this meeting going."

Ignoring this, Mrs. Pargeter rode on. "Yes, I think everyone's got secrets." Then, suddenly seeing a way of staging her "heroics," she continued, musing, "Maybe that's what was in Theresa Cotton's notebook . . ."

"Notebook?" Sue Curle repeated sharply.

"Yes," said Mrs. Pargeter, improvising like mad, "I found this notebook of hers only a couple of days ago. Stuck behind a radiator in the hall," she added, remembering the late Mr. Pargeter's instruction always to incorporate as much truth as possible into anything one said. "It had got a list of all your names, all the women who live in Smithy's Loam."

"Oh?" asked Fiona Burchfield-Brown, more curious than alarmed. Goodness, how phoney her accent sounded to Mrs. Pargeter now she knew the truth. Not real cut glass, more like the cheap stuff that gets given away with petrol.

"Yes, I thought it was strange." Mrs. Pargeter chuckled ingenuously. "Pretty funny idea, isn't it, keeping notes on your neighbours?"

"What sort of notes?" asked Carole Temple, tight-lipped. "What did the book say about us?"

"Ah . . ." Mrs. Pargeter hesitated for a moment. She should have thought this through. The question had been inevitable and she hadn't prepared a way of dealing with it. Then she had an inspiration. "Well, I don't know, you see. Your names are all written out in block capitals, but the rest of the stuff's in shorthand."

"And you don't read shorthand?" asked Vivvi Sprake anxiously.

"Oh, what? No, no," Mrs. Pargeter replied, over-acting to give the impression, to those who would take it that way, that she might be lying.

"Well, I'm sure it's not important." Sue Curle spoke evenly, in her hostess role, trying to dismiss the subject. "Now perhaps we ought to get on with—"

"What are you going to do with it?" Jane Watson's voice was sudden and tense, too loud compared to the others.

"I'm not sure," Mrs. Pargeter replied, exaggerating her casualness. "I suppose I really should give it to the police."

"There's no need to do that!" Jane Watson shrieked.

"No," snapped Carole Temple. "Completely unnecessary."

"I wouldn't really bother the police," said Fiona Burchfield-Brown in a more reasonable tone. "I mean, they've always got so much on their plates, and in this case, having decided who killed Theresa—"

"We don't know they have decided that," Mrs. Pargeter interjected.

"No, but it seems a reasonable assumption that they have," Fiona continued, "and I'm sure, much as they would appreciate your public-spiritedness if you did give the notebook to them, they wouldn't really have the time to deal with it."

"Maybe not . . ." Mrs. Pargeter appeared to vacillate. "Mind you, they did ask me to get in touch if I found anything in the house that looked important . . ."

"Oh, I'm sure it's not important," said Vivvi Sprake brightly. "Just an old shorthand notebook."

"I'm not sure. I think it could be *very* important," asserted Mrs. Pargeter, fuelling the suspicions of anyone who thought that perhaps she *could* read shorthand, after all.

"Well, the police are never that pleased about having their time wasted," Sue Curle advised.

Mrs. Pargeter nodded. "True. On the other hand, I think I probably *should* give it to them. Yes," she concluded, reaching a decision, "I'll take it down to the local station tomorrow morning."

There was a silence among the women of Smithy's Loam. Each one looked as if she might be about to break that silence, but each one thought better of it.

It was their hostess who spoke eventually. "Well, perhaps we ought to get on with what we came here for. I mean, this business of the proposed Indian restaurant just on the corner of Smithy's Loam . . ."

There were murmurs and mumbles as they all settled down to discuss the issue.

"There's an important thing I'd like to say before we

start," Sue Curle continued, "and that is that any objections I'm raising to this proposed development have nothing to do with the fact that it's an *Indian* restaurant being proposed. I mean, I'm not against it on racial grounds, I'm against it on environmental grounds."

There were murmurs of middle-class approval for these sentiments. Carole Temple then went off into a paean of praise for all the advantages of Smithy's Loam, its delightful rural aspect, its proximity to so many amenities, its sense of community.

Mrs. Pargeter reflected that she still had to see some evidence of this last quality, but she hadn't time to stay and argue. Having set up her challenge somewhat impetuously, she now had to go and organise her protection.

She saw it like this. The murderer was bound to appear at "Acapulco" some time before the next morning, with the intention at least of appropriating Theresa Cotton's mythical notebook of secrets (though, given the murderer's track record, Mrs. Pargeter was afraid the intention might be more extreme, not to say terminal).

So it was necessary to ensure that, when the murderer arrived, Mrs. Pargeter was ready for her.

She knew she was safe for at least an hour, probably two. The murderer would not want to draw attention to herself by leaving before the end of the meeting and, as discussion about cooking smells and litter and property values grew more intense, it was clear that that would come later rather than sooner.

"Oh, heavens!" said Mrs. Pargeter, interrupting Vivvi Sprake in full flood on the revolting nature of curry smells (revolting from the environmental rather than the racial point of view, of course). "I've just realised I've left a casserole in the oven! It'll be burnt to a cinder! I must dash across and see what's happened!"

So, with many hurried apologies, Mrs. Pargeter made good her escape.

Or at least her escape out of the frying-pan.

CHAPTER THIRTY-EIGHT

"That's all right, Mrs. Pargeter," said Truffler Mason, rueful as ever. "You did right to call me. I'll be over within the hour. You're sure there's no danger of anyone coming earlier?"

"No, they'll be locked in that meeting for a long time yet. For the people of Smithy's Loam, even murder takes second place to a threat to property values."

He let out a small, melancholy laugh. "You know you shouldn't have done this, though, don't you?"

"Well . . ."

"I told you to watch the old heroics, didn't I?"

"Yes, I know, but—"

"I mean, if anything happened to you, Mrs. Pargeter, I'd never be able to look myself in the face again. After

all the things I promised your late husband, I'd feel terrible
if—"

"Don't think about it, Truffler. Nothing *is* going to
happen to me. All that's going to happen is that between
us we're going to catch a murderer."

"Yes." There was a reflective pause from the other end
of the line, and when Truffler spoke again, there was a
new, unfamiliar quality in his voice. "You know, Mrs.
Pargeter, I haven't felt like this since the last job I done
with your husband."

"Like what?"

"Sort of . . . excited. Mr. Pargeter always had that abil-
ity of making things seem fun. And you know what, Mrs.
Pargeter—you got just the same thing going for you!"

Yes, there was no doubt about it. Truffler Mason
sounded positively cheerful.

Mrs. Pargeter felt very secure in the knowledge that her
minder was on his way, but she still thought she ought to
check out other means of protection.

The late Mr. Pargeter, though the most pacific of men,
had had no illusions about the regrettably violent climate
of the modern world and it was for that reason that, at
times, he had felt obliged to carry a gun. Though of course
he never used it, he recognised its occasional usefulness as
a deterrent to the uncharitable intentions of others. (The
nature of his work did not always allow him to be as
selective in his choice of business associates as he might
have wished.)

This small handgun, along with the extensive network
of lavish financial arrangements specified in his will, he
had bequeathed to his beloved wife.

Mrs. Pargeter, though even less likely ever to use it than

her husband, appreciated the legacy. At times, like the present one, it gave her a warm comforting glow to know that, tucked beneath the exotic silks of her underwear drawer, lay that small amulet against the forces of evil.

So her confidence mounted as she reached through her expensive lingerie. With Truffler arriving in an hour, and with the gun in her handbag, she would have nothing to fear from anyone.

It wasn't there.

She checked and rechecked, scrabbling with growing feverishness through the slipperiness of the drawer's contents.

Still nothing.

She pulled the drawer out, turned it over and dumped its shining riches on to the bedroom floor.

There was no gun.

Mrs. Pargeter did not panic. Panic she recognised to be time-wasting and inefficient, and it was a temptation to which she almost never succumbed.

But the situation was undeniably serious. Assuming that the gun had not been mislaid, its absence meant that it had been removed by someone. And that someone was most probably the murderer of Theresa Cotton.

So the murderer had a key to "Acapulco." Perhaps not such a difficult thing to obtain, considering the amount of mutual plant-watering that went on while the residents of Smithy's Loam took their holidays.

More seriously, the removal of the gun revealed Mrs. Pargeter's adversary to be some steps ahead of her. Mrs. Pargeter thought she had only alerted the murderer to her suspicions by her mention of the spurious notebook a few minutes earlier. But the absent gun told a different story.

The swordstick!

Suddenly she remembered it and scrabbled a chair into position against her cupboards. She opened the top one and reached in, her hand feeling along the uncluttered surface.

With a sickening access of understanding, she realised that she was not going to find the swordstick either.

Someone had been inside "Acapulco" and made preparations. The house had been searched thoroughly for weapons.

The murderer was a long way ahead of her.

At that moment, she heard the back door open. She knew it had been locked. The intruder was using a key.

Drawn by the sound of soft footsteps below, and mirroring them with her own, Mrs. Pargeter moved across the bedroom to the landing.

Standing back from the top of the stairs, she could see a little triangle of the hallway.

She held her breath as the figure of a woman crossed that triangle, moving silently from the kitchen to the sitting-room.

And Mrs. Pargeter saw who had killed Theresa Cotton.

CHAPTER THIRTY-NINE

~~~~~~

There was nowhere to hide.

As if drawn by magnetism, Mrs. Pargeter found herself walking down the stairs towards her adversary. At their foot she stopped and saw the murderer pause behind the tall outline of an armchair. Mrs. Pargeter's favourite armchair.

It was then that she saw the naked blade of the swordstick in the murderer's hand. She saw that hand withdrawn, ready to plunge into the back of the armchair.

"Stop," said Mrs. Pargeter calmly, "I'm not there. And I don't really want to have to have it re-upholstered."

The murderer swung round to face her and, again drawing back the sword, advanced.

Mrs. Pargeter stood her ground at the foot of the stairs

and, with a confidence she didn't feel, said, "You can kill me if you like. Obviously, I can't stop you. But all you'll achieve by that is stopping me from taking Theresa Cotton's notebook to the police in the morning. You won't have the notebook itself."

The murderer had stopped her advance, and stood, listening.

Emboldened, Mrs. Pargeter continued, "And, without my help, you won't find it. If you kill me straight away, you could search the house all night and still not find that notebook."

Little did the murderer know how true that was. There was a kind of satisfaction in the thought of the murderer turning the whole house upside down looking for something that didn't exist. But the satisfaction of the thought was considerably reduced when Mrs. Pargeter reflected that it could only be realised after her own murder.

"The police, on the other hand," Mrs. Pargeter went on, "are experts in searching for clues. And, if my body was found here—or even traces of it—they'd certainly subject this house to one of their most thorough searches. I don't think there's any doubt that they'd find the notebook. And, of course, it'd be a simple matter for them to have the shorthand deciphered. And then they'd know what it was that Theresa Cotton found out about you—the truth that she confronted you with when she came round to your house the evening she died."

"Where is the notebook?" the murderer hissed, once again threatening with the swordstick.

Mrs. Pargeter moved forward. "Oh, don't worry, I'll tell you all about the notebook. In time. Now shall we go into the sitting-room and have a little talk . . . ?"

Open-mouthed, the murderer watched as Mrs. Pargeter

moved past her in a stately manner and went to sit on the sofa. Ever the gracious hostess, Mrs. Pargeter waved to the big armchair. "Please . . ."

With bad grace, the murderer sat down.

"I suppose you heard what I said about the notebook from behind the hatch . . . ?"

The murderer nodded.

"I have to confess, it never occurred to me that it might be you, Kirsten," Mrs. Pargeter apologised. "You see, I was under the impression that only Sue was in the house the evening when Theresa called. That you were out. That's what Sue told me."

"But Sue was—"

Mrs. Pargeter raised a magisterial hand for silence. "No, I've worked it out now. I should have realised before. Sue was lying. You were the one who was there and she was the one who was out. Out with her lover, of course, with Geoff. But she didn't want anyone to know about their affair, so when I asked if she'd been in when Theresa called, rather than raise questions about her absence, she said yes. She'd been in, you'd been out. And when the police started interrogating her, the lie became even firmer."

"She thought she could keep the affair quiet," said Kirsten, her vowels even more deformed than usual by contempt, "from her husband."

"Yes, but you knew about it, didn't you?"

The Norwegian girl shrugged. "Maybe."

"Oh, you did. And you used the knowledge to blackmail Sue."

"How do you mean?"

"That's why you never did any work for her. You were useless as an *au pair*, never lifted a finger. But she didn't dare get rid of you until her divorce was sorted out, in case you spilled the beans about Geoff. And the arrangement suited you very well, because it allowed you time to get on with your main business."

"I don't know what you're talking about."

Mrs. Pargeter didn't quite know what she was talking about herself, but as she went on, she found everything got clearer. Her mind was working well, seeing relationships between previously unregarded details, building up little chains of logic and joining them together into longer chains.

"I'm talking about drugs," she hazarded.

The girl in the armchair stiffened, telling Mrs. Pargeter that she had hit a bull's-eye.

"Nice little set-up you'd got here. Cocaine mostly, wasn't it? Easy enough to buy the stuff in the London clubs you were always going to. Easy enough to send it back to Norway in those many letters you kept sending back. And maybe a little local dealing for anyone who wanted it . . . Like Rod Cotton, for instance . . . Fitted his Yuppie image, didn't it, cocaine?"

"So what if you're right?" asked Kirsten sourly. "I don't think the knowledge is going to do you much good." She waved the swordstick menacingly. "Come on, where is this notebook?"

"Oh, I'm not ready to tell you yet," said Mrs. Pargeter with a complacent smile.

Kirsten rose from her chair. "Then maybe I'll have to make you tell me . . ."

"Torture? Hmm, it might take a long time. And of course you always might kill me by mistake. Or suppose I screamed . . . ? I have rather a loud scream, you know. Neighbours might notice."

"I have to get that notebook, and I'll be getting it by

whichever method it is needed," said Kirsten, sinisterly ungrammatical.

"I'll tell you the best way of getting it."

"What's that?"

"It is for you to wait till I give it to you."

"Don't be silly, old woman!"

"No, listen. I will give it to you, I promise. And I won't say any more about it . . ." Mrs. Pargeter smiled ingenuously, *"on the understanding* that you won't hurt me. OK? My side of the bargain is that I give you the notebook—your side of the bargain is that then you leave the house and I'm not hurt at all."

"OK," said Kirsten. "That's a deal."

What kind of naïve old idiot does she think I am, Mrs. Pargeter wondered. If her past behaviour's anything to go by, only a few seconds would elapse between my handing over the notebook (assuming, of course, it existed) and her running me through with the swordstick.

"All right. Where is the notebook?" Kirsten went on.

"I'll tell you. But in a minute. I just want to check out first if I'm right about how you killed Theresa Cotton."

Kirsten shrugged and looked at her watch. "Five minutes, then you give me the book. Or . . ." She waved the swordstick meaningfully.

Yes, thought Mrs. Pargeter, this girl really must have written me off as stupid, if she thinks I think she'll let me survive once I've spelled out the details of her crime. Still, it's all helping in my current game of playing for time.

"Right, this is the way I see it, Kirsten. You supplied cocaine to Rod, probably while he still had a job, and then certainly during that spell after he lost his job. You used to come over to the house here."

240

Suddenly she saw how she had misinterpreted Carole Temple's references to someone younger coming to "Acapulco" while Rod was there, someone with two children to look after. She had assumed that had meant Vivvi, but in fact it had been Kirsten. And their dealings had not been in sex, but in drugs.

"So?" said Kirsten. She was bored and looked at her watch.

"When Theresa came to the house and said she knew about your cocaine-dealing, you thought she was about to shop you to the police. Which was why you decided you had to kill her.

"Easy enough to do. You could go out of the back of 'Perigord' and round by the path to the garden gate of this house. Sue had been given a key when she came in to water the plants. Maybe you used that, maybe you'd had a copy made . . . anyway, that was how you got in then —and how you got in tonight, come to that. When you got Rod's tie I don't know, but it wouldn't have been difficult.

"So you came in, strangled Theresa—she gave no resistance because you caught her by surprise . . . she probably even obligingly died on the polythene sheet she was using for packing her belongings. Then you sealed up her body in the convenient polythene, put it in the freezer and locked it.

"And of course you found a nice little bonus here, didn't you? Two thousand pounds, very handy. Have a nice few days shopping on that.

"Hmm . . ." Mrs. Pargeter smiled grimly. "It was using the freezer that should have made me realise it was you."

"What you mean?" asked Kirsten, with her first flicker of interest.

"Well, hiding the body that way was risky. It would have been discovered at some time—after the six months of prepaid storage, if not before. So the person who killed Theresa had to be someone prepared for that risk, someone who knew that within six months—in your case, less, two months—they'd be out of the country.

"Anyway, there's another reason I should have worked out it was you."

"What?"

"The murderer also had to be someone who knew Rod's real situation, who knew he was out of a job. And I think he kept in touch with you during the six months after he left here."

"Why should he do that?" the girl asked languidly.

"For the same reason he'd made contact with you in the first place. Cocaine. I think, whenever he had some money during that dreadful decline, he would get in touch with you to buy more of the stuff."

"Maybe," Kirsten acknowledged.

Another hideous piece of the jigsaw fell into place. "And I think that's why he died," said Mrs. Pargeter softly.

"What do you mean?"

"For the last time in his life, he had money. Oh, what a fool I was—I gave him a hundred pounds. And he wanted to spend it on cocaine, so he rang you, and—" Mrs. Pargeter's thoughts accelerated. "Oh, my God, yes. I remember, when I got back from seeing him, Sue had just had to come back from work, so that you could go out. Some excuse . . . what was it? Oh yes, visa ran out, you had to go to the Norwegian Embassy. I don't think you went anywhere near the Norwegian Embassy that day."

"No? And where do you think I did go?" the girl asked coolly.

"I think you went to the Embankment and found Rod. I think maybe you waited till the evening—it would have been easier in the evening—and then you asked him to walk down towards the river to do your deal. And I think when you reached the parapet of the river, you pushed him over it."

"It is possible," Kirsten conceded. "You could never prove it."

"Oh, I don't need to prove it. This is only for my own satisfaction," said Mrs. Pargeter, again donning her mantle of bumbling naïveté. "Remember, I'm never going to breathe a word of this to anyone. Once I've given you the notebook, I forget all about the whole business. Right?"

"Right," said Kirsten, with an unpleasant smile. She took another look at her watch. "Now, the notebook, please."

Mrs. Pargeter felt a little chill of fear. There was a finite amount of time she could spend pretending to look for a fictitious notebook, and she didn't want to put Kirsten's patience to too much of a test. She had a feeling the results might be rather unpleasant.

Play for a little more time, though, before she started the search. "Yes, just before I get the book, Kirsten, tell me, am I right?"

"Right?"

"Right about the two murders."

The Norwegian girl jutted out her lower lip and wobbled her head contemplatively from side to side. "Near enough right," she said eventually.

243

"Oh, good," said Mrs. Pargeter.

"And now, no more wasting time. Where is this note-book?"

"Um . . ."

"Come on, quickly. I have a plane to catch tonight."

"Are you going back to Norway?"

"No. Not that it's any of your business, but I go first to Paris. Then South America."

"Oh?"

"I have many friends there. You see, you did not get all the details right. I did not just buy drugs casually at London clubs. I am part of a larger network."

"Based in South America?"

"Yes. And since I think Europe is not too good for me for a little while, I go to South America. My friends will look after me."

"Oh, I see."

"Now, the notebook . . ."

Mrs. Pargeter looked at her blankly.

"The notebook." The swordstick was once again bran-dished. "You know, I think I would be prepared to risk a little torture if—"

"Oh, no, no. It'll be all right, I'll—" Suddenly Mrs. Pargeter was immobilised by a burst of coughing. It seemed to fill the room.

Which was just as well, because, as it had been intended to do, the coughing covered the sounds of Truffler Mason's approach.

Indeed, Kirsten was only aware that he was in the house when suddenly her arms were pinioned from behind her chair. The swordstick fell, clattering on to the tiles in front of the fireplace.

The murderer struggled, but was held as effectively as

244

by a straitjacket. A stream of Norwegian obscenities flooded from her mouth.

Mrs. Pargeter rose from the sofa and patted her hair into place. "Well, I'm very glad to see you, Truffler," she understated.

CHAPTER FORTY

The police were called, and Kirsten's threatening of Mrs.
Pargeter with a swordstick, witnessed by Truffler Mason,
was sufficient for them to arrest her. The suggestion of a
cocaine-dealing connection prompted searches in "Perigord," where enough evidence was found to break up a
considerable drug-smuggling network. Then, under interrogation, the Norwegian girl confessed to the murders of
Theresa and Rod Cotton.

In fact, the general assumption that the police had been
satisfied with a husband-kills-wife explanation of the first
murder was untrue. The case had remained very much
open, and at the time of Kirsten's arrest, the police enquiries had still been progressing. At their own pace.

A pace which, Mrs. Pargeter noted with quiet satisfaction, was rather slower than her own.

The surface of life in Smithy's Loam soon closed over the murders; all appeared as it always had appeared. And no doubt, beneath that gleaming surface, the old secrets were joined by new secrets, and all those secrets, in the cause of middle-class gentility, were kept secret.

The planning application for the Indian restaurant was, incidentally, turned down. But when, a couple of months later, another application was filed to turn the same premises into an up-market French restaurant, there was unaccountably no opposition from local residents.

The lives of the daytime denizens of Smithy's Loam went on much as before.

At "High Bushes" Fiona and Alexander Burchfield-Brown still tried to live up to their false standards, and Fiona spent much of her time agonising over her next, inevitable lapse from those standards.

In "Perigord" at least there was a happy ending. Her husband's rearguard action against their divorce settlement having been finally exhausted, Sue Curle got the hoped-for custody of her children. She did not engage another *au pair*, arranging instead to spend more time at home, to fit her work around the children's school and holiday commitments. And the frequency with which her boss, Geoff, had to come and consult her while she was at home suggested that he might, in time, take up more permanent residence.

At "Haymakers" the ending was less traditionally happy. Vivvi Sprake discovered that her husband Nigel was having yet another affair with yet another secretary and realised finally that that was just the sort of man he was. She was then faced with a decision. Should she make a fuss and challenge the stability of their marriage? Or should she quietly accept the situation and keep an eye open for the kind of diversion for which her brief encounter with Rod Cotton had given her an incipient taste? She opted for the second alternative, and her children had a lifetime supply of motel soap.

In "Hibiscus" Jane Watson slowly came out of her shell. Though the shock of her fears about Theresa Cotton and Mrs. Pargeter had put her back in a terrifying way, she had even at that time been emerging from the breakdown, and with each day that separated her from her stay at the Church of Utter Simplicity, she got better. Beginning with short, informal coffee mornings at Mrs. Pargeter's, she soon began to lose her fear of people and start to lead a more normal social life. And her recovery may well have been speeded by the news that the Church of Utter Simplicity had been closed down after police investigation into its financial affairs.

Inside "Cromarty" Carole Temple still found deep fulfillment in her relentless persecution of specks of dust. And if her husband's unusual sartorial tastes ever caused any discord in their marriage, it was not visible through the house's highly polished windows.

And at "Acapulco," Mrs. Pargeter, her life animated by regular chauffeur-driven trips to London, worked out the six months which she had promised herself to spend in Smithy's Loam.

With the firm intention that, at the end of that six months, she would move on.